I0734853

ZACK

M. MALONE

Editor: Daisycakes Creative Services

Proofreader: Leah Guinan

CrushStar Romance

An Imprint of CrushStar Multimedia LLC

Ebook ISBN-13: 978-1-938789-24-3

Print ISBN-13: 978-1-938789-25-0

Contents

- Contemporary Romance -

Blue-Collar Billionaires

Billions from the deadbeat dad they never knew sounds pretty sweet. Until they find out what he really wants.

Tank / Finn / Gabe / Zack / Luke

The Alexanders

One More Day : "Good girl" Ridley has always attracted bad guys. Now she's on the run and has nowhere to hide. So when Jackson Alexander mistakes her for her twin, she decides to do something she knows is wrong. *She lies.*

The Things I Do for You : Nicholas Alexander finally has something the woman of his dreams needs. He'll give Raina a baby if she gives him what he wants. *Her.*

He's the Man : Matt Simmons is over Army doctors poking him until he sees his old babysitter, now a physical therapist, is h-o-t. Suddenly he's seeing the benefits of therapy.

All I Want: The only thing Kaylee wants is for Elliott Alexander to stop treating her like she's invisible. But a car accident forces her to reach out to the only man she trusts to save her.

All I Need is You : When the man she loves leaves town after their steamy kiss, Kaylee Wilhelm is done. But when she's targeted by a stalker, Eli is the only one who can protect her.

Say You Will : Mara Simmons has always known Trent Townsend is *The One*. But when she suspects his frequent business trips have *nothing* to do with business, she sets in motion a chain of events bigger than she can imagine and discovers that the man she loves just might be a stranger.

Just One Thing : Scientist Bennett Alexander is a bona fide genius but he still can't figure out how to "get the girl". So he hires a dating tutor. What could go wrong? Other than falling for his teacher, of course.

Bad King: My parents just put a gold diggers target on my back. But if all they want is a wedding, I can do that. I'll find the fiancee of their nightmares. *Who Wants to Marry a Billionaire? Must be completely inappropriate.*

Bad Blood : I'd do anything for my best friend's little sister. Until she asks for the one thing I can't give. One night. No rules. ***2019 RITA® Award Winner!***

- Romantic Suspense -

(Co-authored with Nana Malone)

- The Shameless Trilogy
- The Force Duet
- The Deep Duet
- The Sin Duet
- The Brazen Duet

ZACK

Chapter One

Zack

There was a time when I thought my brother was invincible. He could run faster, throw farther and hit harder than I ever could.

He was my hero.

I was always the loner, the antisocial misfit with few friends and even fewer fucks to give. Whereas Gabe is the type of guy who can charm the pants off a nun and makes everything look easy.

I glance over at my brother and have to acknowledge that his life hasn't been so charmed lately. His face is pale and sweaty from exertion. One arm is slung over my shoulders as we shuffle down the hall at a snail's pace and I'm pretty sure my grip is the only thing keeping him upright. He looks terrible.

Well, to be fair he looks like a guy who just got stabbed.

Once we reach his bedroom, he lets out a ragged sigh as I help him sit down on the bed. It only took so much effort to get him back up the stairs because he's determined to prove he doesn't need my help. His superman act has definitely taken a toll. His forehead has a deep furrow and his breathing is shallow.

He was only in the hospital for a few days before checking himself out against medical advice. It's been two weeks since then and I'm getting worried. He doesn't seem to be much better and I can tell he's still in a lot of pain.

"I think it's time for your meds again."

"No more. I can't think when I take that shit." He closes his eyes and doesn't look at me while I cover him with his blankets. Ignoring me while I'm helping him seems to soothe his pride a bit.

"You're a terrible patient." It's impossible to keep the amusement from my voice which just seems to piss him off further.

He cracks his eyes open slightly. "Where's Sasha?"

I grin, knowing the real reason for his grumpiness is more about her absence than the knife wound in his side. "She had to babysit for her sister. Don't worry, she'll be back before your heart breaks."

"Fuck off." There's no heat behind the curse though and that worries me more than anything else he's said or done today.

We've had some pretty heavy stuff thrown at us lately and I'm not sure how he's handling it. I've been vacillating between enraged and depressed over the past few days myself.

"How is he?"

We both turn at the sound of Sasha's voice. I manage to get out of the way, barely, as Sasha pushes past me and climbs on the bed next to Gabe. The frown lines on his forehead ease immediately.

"I'll be downstairs if you need me."

Neither of them looks up as I leave but I don't take offense. Now that Sasha's here I can finally take a deep breath and relax a little. As much as I love my brother, he's always been one step away from straying from the straight and narrow. Worrying about him is as much a part of my life as breathing.

We grew up under unusual circumstances when our mothers, best friends before being knocked up by the same guy, decided to raise us together. Our community is small and there were plenty of people here who thought our little family didn't belong. I doubt I would have been popular anyway as scrawny and sickly as I was but our social status definitely affected Gabe. He has a natural propensity for trouble but watching our moms struggle to pay the bills gave him the push he needed to develop some of his less than legal skills.

After repeated brushes with the law as a teenager, it's been a constant battle to keep him away from temptation. I truly believe it was only the worry about upsetting our mothers that kept him out of jail. Now that he's with Sasha, I don't worry so much anymore. Even if he was tempted back to his old life, he wouldn't do anything that would take him away from her.

As I close the door behind me, Debbie straightens up from where she was leaning against the wall.

"Hey, Mom. How long have you been out here?"

She smiles and glances behind me at the closed door. "I wanted to check on him before I go. But I won't disturb him if he's resting."

Ever since Gabe was attacked, both of our mothers have been hovering to the point where they were driving him crazy. My mom is the type that doesn't take hints too well but Debbie has always tried to respect our boundaries. Even when it's hard for her to do.

"He's doing a little better." I lie, hoping it will put her mind at ease. "Now that Sasha is back, maybe he'll stop being difficult and just take his pain pills."

She pulls me into a hug. "Thank you, sweetheart. I don't know what we would have done without you and Sasha these past few weeks."

Her head barely grazes my chin but she smells like lavender and just... home. Growing up, both Gabe and I got used to being scooped up for "snuggles" as she calls it. Technically she's Gabe's mom but she's never treated me like anything other than a second son. Getting comfort from Debbie is the most natural thing in the world. It's so weird now as an adult to realize that sometimes she needs comfort, too.

She pulls back and dabs at her eyes with the back of her hand. "I finished your laundry and Paula is out getting groceries."

"You didn't have to do that."

She waves that away. "We need to do something."

I understand that completely. Anything is better than sitting around and feeling helpless.

"Anyway, I just wanted to make sure that you check on Josie from time to time."

Just the sound of her name hits me like a physical slap. "Jo's here? Where is she?"

I didn't hear her come in so she must have arrived while I was trying to wrestle Gabe up the stairs.

"She's outside. Painting."

"Oh." I don't need to hear anything else. "I'll take care of it."

Debbie squeezes my arm before walking back down the stairs. I hear her walking around and then the slam of the front door closing and still I stand there. I'm not ready to deal with what's next. Taking care of Gabe these past few weeks has been a challenge but even that doesn't compare to what I'm about to do. Because as difficult as it's been to see my brother hurt, I've also had to deal with the only other person who has the capacity to annoy and terrify me the same way he does.

The girl who has loved him forever.

———

As soon as I walk through the back door, I see her. She's wearing faded denim coveralls and her long, dark hair is up in a messy bun. I can only see her from behind but that face is burned into my memory. The dark slash of her eyebrows, the dramatic upturned brown eyes and the pouty mouth that has fueled so many of my fantasies.

I swallow hard, disgusted by myself. Shame has been a constant companion ever since discovering that I have a bit of a *thing* for my brother's old girlfriend. We've all been friends so long that Jo is almost like a second sibling. She's been trailing along after Gabe for years and I've practically watched her grow up.

Which makes me feel even more like a pervert for suddenly noticing that Josephine Harlow is insanely hot.

I'm so busy berating myself it takes almost a full minute before the destruction around me registers. When Debbie said she was painting, I knew I needed to get down here. Josie's an artist but she prefers photography. She only paints when she's upset.

The first week after Gabe's attack, she came over every day to check on him. Afterward, she'd come out here and paint. She didn't say anything to me and she didn't cry. She just stood in front of the easel and painted until all the light was gone. It filled me with rage and helplessness every time to see her hurting like that, knowing there was nothing I could do.

But this is... different.

Paint is everywhere. She's covered in it and so is my brother's backyard. It looks like she bought several cans of paint and then blew them up one by one. When she leans down and sticks her hands directly into an open canister, I realize that isn't too far off. She's painting but she's doing it in the most haphazard way possible, flinging it at the canvas in front of her with quick, angry swipes.

"I can really see the emotion in your work."

Josie freezes mid-swing and the paint on her hands lands with a soft plop in the grass.

"Oh, hey." She looks down at her hands like she isn't sure where all the paint came from. Her cheeks flush pink and she sticks her hands in her pockets. "How long have you been standing there?"

"Long enough to wonder who the hell is going to clean all this up."

Her eyes narrow. "Bite me, Zack."

Then her eyes latch onto mine and before I can stop myself, my arms are open. She launches herself at me, knocking into me so hard that I have to take a step back to keep us upright. There's paint all over me now but I don't even care. The only thing that matters is the way her shoulders are shaking beneath my hands. In that moment, all I care about is the fact that she's hurting.

Her feelings for my brother have never been a secret. Ever since that terrible day when Gabe interrupted the assholes who were trying to take advantage of her at a party, she's looked at him like he's her personal hero. Most people assume Josie loves Gabe for the same reasons everyone else does. Because he's handsome and charming and the kind of guy that girls like her dream of. They have no idea that she sees him as her own personal guardian angel.

But I do.

Everyone around us doesn't know the circumstances behind it because as far as I know, none of us ever told anyone about what happened that night.

As much as Gabe and I wanted to go back and tear those guys apart, Josie was frantic. She was humiliated and frightened about what her parents and friends would say and think. She didn't want anyone to know and so that night has become just one more thing that none of us speak of. Jo has been following us around ever since and after a while she blended seamlessly into the fabric of our lives. It should be strange how we adopted her, like a random puppy or something.

But she just fit with us.

"I finally got him upstairs. He just needs to sleep. You know nothing can keep Gabe down for long."

Her fingers curl into my chest, balling the fabric of my cotton T-shirt beneath her fists. She rubs her face against my shirt and nods wordlessly. The helplessness I felt earlier comes back full force.

"It's all going to be okay." I'm stroking her hair, whispering whatever I think will help to calm her down. But inside, I'm on fire because I know his injury isn't the only reason she's crying. It's because Josie can't do what she really wants and watch over Gabe herself.

He has a girlfriend now and things are never going to be the same.

After a few minutes she pulls back and wipes at her tears, leaving a streak of red paint on her cheek.

"I'm okay now. Sorry about that." She can't even look at me. Her breaths are still coming in gasping little sobs as she rolls up the paper on the easel.

I want to help her but something tells me she won't welcome that so I move out of the way so she can collect the brushes near my feet. Several locks of her wavy hair have escaped her bun and are sticking to the paint on her cheeks and neck. Even sweaty and disheveled, she's the most beautiful woman I've ever seen.

Over the years I've watched her blossom from a scared, naive young girl into a confident woman. The outside may have changed but she's still our same sweet Josie on the inside. And she still loves the man who saved her when no one else cared. All the guys she's dated since high school seemed like plastic stand-ins for my brother. I think our parents and hers have secretly been waiting for them to get back together. Hell, even I was expecting it to happen eventually.

Now things are different and it's like she's self-destructing right in front of me.

"You don't have to apologize. I'm worried about him, too."

She looks up at me sharply. "You are? Is there something you aren't telling me?"

"No, it's not that. He's just never gotten hurt so badly before."

"Yeah." Her eyes become distant and she looks out over the yard. "He's been better lately. Less impulsive. I thought I wouldn't have to worry about him anymore."

I understand exactly what she means. Gabe has gotten into his fair share of trouble, and so have I, but most of it was borne of necessity. When money was tight we'd boost a few cars to make sure the gas wasn't cut off in the middle of winter. The stuff we did was wrong but I've never regretted it because we did what we had to do. Gabe though, he always seemed to *enjoy* it. Now that we've inherited millions from our father, it shouldn't even be an issue. But for a while

I was still worried that he'd be drawn back to his old ways just for the rush.

Thinking of our wayward billionaire father reminds me of the reason Gabe is upstairs wounded in the first place. I push that thought away. I can't even think about his part in all this or I'll get pissed off all over again.

Josie grabs the easel and folds it closed gently. "I should go home and clean up. My mom's expecting me to drop by later. I can't let her see me like this."

Her mother is a real piece of work. No doubt she'd shit a brick if she saw her daughter dressed like a mechanic and covered in paint. Her mother tolerates Gabe, even she can't resist him, but she's never bothered to hide her disgust for me.

"Make sure to give Geraldine my regards."

Her mouth tilts up slightly. "I'll do that. And Zack... thanks." She ducks her head bashfully before scooping up the paint.

I watch her walk away, her pert little bottom twitching attractively even under the ugly coveralls she's wearing. She doesn't look back, probably forgetting that I'm here as soon as her back is turned. I've never fooled myself about my place in Josie's life. In her world it's all Gabe, all the time and I've never thought differently. It's only recently that I've realized the toll I've paid along the way. It takes a little chunk out of me every time I have to dry her tears after he hurts her. But I can't stop. Because I love them both.

Everyone thinks mortality is about the sudden loss of the soul. We live our lives fearing the worst that we think can happen. Car accident. Gun shot. Heart attack. But very few people know the truth, that those aren't the worst ways you can go. Although painful, at least a bullet to the heart is quick.

Watching Josie pine for someone who will never want her the way I do feels like dying slowly.

———

After Josie leaves, I pull out my phone and tap on the contact for one of my newfound brothers, Tank.

He answers right away. "Zack. I had a feeling you'd be calling today."

"I would have called earlier but it took longer to get Gabe settled than I thought."

"Is he still bitching about that little scratch on the side?"

I burst out laughing. Tank was a sniper for years and he's still a pretty scary dude. I've no doubt he's seen and survived way worse.

"I'll definitely tell him you said that."

Tank is quiet for a moment then says, "I'll never forget the moment I realized he'd been stabbed. I lost about ten years off my life that day. That was a brave thing he did. Stupid but brave."

Thinking of the guy responsible for my brother's hospital stay sends a shaft of fear straight to my heart.

Blade.

We assumed he was connected to our father's shady past but we had no idea what we were dealing with. Gabe broke into the warehouse Blade was staying in and had the terrible judgment to bring along a friend of his from the old days. A friend who stole something when Gabe wasn't looking.

He had no idea what had happened until Sasha's house was trashed and he got the message Blade left for him. A dagger through her picture. To protect her, Gabe confronted him and ended up learning firsthand how he earned his name.

Tank clears his throat sounding surprisingly emotional. "Anyway, I got in touch with the guy you told me about. He admitted to stealing the ring but I got it back. I gave it to Max. He said he'll handle it. Hopefully dear old Dad is actually telling the truth for once."

Well, that's a relief. Hopefully Max will settle whatever business they have and convince Blade to go back home. The last thing we need is that scary bastard hanging around. Tank agrees and by the time we hang up, I breathe deeply for the first time since I saw Gabe in that hospital bed.

Finally. A little peace.

I go back upstairs, careful to be quiet as I pass Gabe's door. At this point he should be sleeping so even though I feel like I should check on him, I don't. Sasha's taking care of him so I'm not needed there. That gives me a little pang behind the heart.

I really like her but it's strange to think of someone else being closer to my brother than I am. It leaves me with a sense of being out of place somehow. When Gabe bought this house, he convinced me that it was ridiculous to buy my own place right away. Why not wait until I found something I actually wanted and just stay with him until then?

It made sense at the time but I think it's time to revisit the buying my own place situation. Sasha hasn't been in my brother's life for long but I already know where things are heading. When a man looks at a woman like she's more vital than the air he breathes, only an idiot wouldn't lock it down with a ring. She'll be my sister before the end of the year, I'm willing to bet. My brother is many things but never an idiot. His recent behavior not withstanding.

I don't want to cramp their style or feel like a third wheel but those aren't the only reasons I want to move out.

Gabe has always been more popular and charming and the one everyone likes. And I've never minded before because I love him. Maybe that's what makes this situation so unbearable. I never thought that I would envy or resent him for anything he has.

But when I look at Josie, when I see the love shining out of her eyes that he so easily disregards, it makes me feel something I never thought I could.

It makes me hate him a little bit.

Chapter Two

Josie

I knew where my life was heading until the night my best friend almost died.

My mind flashes to the painful image of Gabe, pale and bruised, with tubes coming out all over. His appearance was shocking enough but then he'd opened his eyes and said something that changed everything. He said, "Make sure she knows I love her, Jo. If I die, make sure Sasha knows."

The nurses had been in the middle of sedating him so I don't even know if he remembers what he said to me. But ever since then what he said hasn't been far from my mind.

What if I were the one in that hospital bed? What would I regret? Would I be satisfied with the things I've accomplished or disappointed by all the time I've wasted?

I've made a lot of decisions over the past few weeks, some that others might call hasty, because of those words. I moved out of my parents' house and broke up with my boyfriend. All because I don't have an answer to any of those questions.

I had a path for my life but it turns out I was just stumbling along the road others paved for me.

I'm not much of a crier but everything seemed to converge into a mass of confusion today when I really looked at my life. I saw the bare bones of who I am and it wasn't a pretty picture. Suddenly all I wanted was to cover that up with some color. Something to bring life to my black and white world.

Of course Zack had to see me in the midst of my breakdown.

Why is it that the one person you most want to impress always sees you at your worst? Zack has been in a unique position these past few years to see me at my lowest points. It's no wonder he looks at me like an annoying little sister. Meanwhile, I'm dreaming of tracing all his tattoos with my tongue. He'd probably be completely disgusted if he knew.

Ugh.

I'm putting away the paint cans and cursing myself for being a complete coward when Sasha finds me. She looks exhausted but happy. Much like Gabe has looked since he met her.

"Hey, I thought I heard your voice earlier." Her eyes widen when she takes in my paint-splattered appearance. "I didn't know you were a painter?"

I grimace, looking down at the damage. "I'm not. This is more like... therapy."

"Ah, I see." Wisely, she doesn't ask any more about it. "I was just coming down to get something to eat. Do you want to join me?"

Her invitation comes as a bit of a surprise. "Sure, I would love that. Just give me a second."

She nods eagerly and then wanders over to look at the brushes and easel in the corner of the shed. I try not to stare at her too obviously as I strip off the coveralls and place them in a plastic bag. We've been friendly lately but she's never sought me out before like this.

Everyone thinks I'm jealous because Gabe has a girlfriend now but I'm happy he has someone who loves him and will be there for him. These strange feelings of loss are just me acknowledging how things will change. For years, he's been my go-to guy when I need something. Now things will be different and that's the way it should be.

Sasha has been incredibly supportive of my photography career and even though I haven't known her long, it's meant a lot to me. Especially since I've been doing a lot of erotic art lately. A lot of people, including my own family, are scandalized and shocked by my pictures so I was worried that she would assume the worst when she found out what kind of pictures I take.

Surprisingly, she came with Gabe to my first show and they later bought one of the prints. It's not hard to understand why he fell for her. Her gorgeous brown skin and curly black hair make her look like she came straight from some exotic island and she has the type of strong personality he needs. Gabe needs a woman who can hold her own.

"Okay, I think that's it."

I press down hard on the lid of each can to be sure they're closed securely and then stack everything on the shelves. When Gabe bought this house, he put this shed back here just for me to store things. I've been hiding my art supplies from my parents since high school. Luckily Debbie and Paula never cared if I left stuff at their house. Now that I'm living with my friend Isabelle, I don't have to bother hiding it anymore. I make a mental note to ask Zack for help loading my car later so I can transport some more of my supplies.

We walk back to the house and Sasha kicks off her shoes once we enter through the back door. I'm so used to being in Gabe's house that I go directly to the kitchen sink to wash the paint from my hands and arms. We fall into an easy rhythm preparing the food. We're just sitting down to eat, when Sasha looks over at me mischievously.

"I actually wanted to ask you something. But feel free to say no if it's weird." Sasha twirls her fork between her fingers, the metal clanking against her plate.

"You're making me nervous. What is it?"

"It's not that big of a deal. I just know someone who had some pictures taken for her boyfriend's birthday and I was wondering if you would consider it. Taking pictures of me. You know, sexy pictures."

Suddenly her discomfort makes sense. Sasha is pretty brazen but this tends to make even the most ballsy women a little shy.

"You want to do boudoir shots?"

"Yes. I mean, I was thinking about it." She lets out a little nervous laugh. "Is that a stupid idea? Too cheesy?"

"Are you kidding? I'm sure there aren't too many guys who would turn down that gift. Gabe would love it."

A relieved smile spreads across her face. "So, you'll do it? I don't think I could take those kinds of pictures with a photographer that I don't know. Plus, all the photos you had on display in the gallery were so classy and intimate."

I cover her hand with mine. "You have nothing to worry about, Sasha. They'll be really tasteful and elegant. You'll see."

I can understand her concern because boudoir shots are tricky. When done well, they're spectacular but when done badly... The results can be anything from tacky to horrifying.

She smiles and squeezes my hand before taking another bite of spaghetti. Then her gaze turns calculating. "Speaking of that day at the gallery, I've been meaning to ask you. How are things with you and Zack?"

I choke slightly and then reach for my water glass. "Fine. Why wouldn't they be?"

She tilts her head. "You know what I mean."

I do unfortunately. When Sasha started dating Gabe, she asked me flat out if there was anything between us. I love Gabe and I would never want to come between the two of them so I was forced to tell her the truth. A truth that very few people know. That Gabe isn't the Marshall brother I want.

"There's nothing going on. He doesn't think of me that way. We've all been friends for so long that I'm like a sister to him."

Sasha chews her food, lost in thought. "The way he looked at you that day in the gallery was not very brotherly."

The sudden burn in the pit of my stomach takes me off guard. It's a dangerous thing, hope. It's exactly what I don't need to be doing, imagining that maybe one day Zack will wake up and realize what I've always known. That we're perfect for each other. It's a fantasy. A dangerous one.

"I probably shouldn't have said anything that day but I wanted you to understand. People always assume that I'm in love with Gabe."

"Does Zack think that, too?"

"Yeah."

She sighs. "This is a mess. Well, for what it's worth, I think you would be really good for him. He's always taking care of everyone else and I think he could use someone looking out for him."

I agree completely but the thing is, Zack doesn't want anyone to look out for him. He's built himself an island and while he might allow me to visit, he's never given any indication that he wants me to stay.

fter that, Sasha and I finish our dinner in relative peace. She's making the effort to keep up the conversation but my mind is only half on what she's saying. The other half is on what Zack is doing up in his room. Probably playing his guitar. He does that when he's stressed. After crying all over him, I can only guess he's making himself scarce. He's surely had his fill of female drama for the day.

Sasha goes back upstairs to check on Gabe and I decide to go straight home, making the decision not to visit my mother today. Spending time with her is a battle of wits even on a good day and I don't have the fortitude right now. When I park in the drive in front of Isabelle's house, I'm suddenly very tired.

The house is a pretty, three story Victorian right in the heart of West Haven. Izzie inherited this house from her grandparents late last year. It has an old-world elegance that's completely different from Izzie's brazen, punk style but somehow it fits her.

We've been friends a long time but I have to admit I was hesitant when she asked me to move in. You never really know someone until you've lived together and I wasn't sure if I wanted to test our friendship that way. Especially since I like things tidy and Izzie has a tendency to be a walking disaster. Her room growing up always looked like a tornado had just come through.

But so far, we've meshed perfectly. Luckily her messiness is mainly confined to her room. She's not a morning person but I've learned that as long as I don't wake her up before ten on the weekends, we can make it work. I get a place to stay for next to nothing and Izzie says she feels better not rattling around this big place all alone.

Anything is better than living with my parents.

When I open the door, Isabelle looks up from her perch on the couch. She's already changed into her favorite leggings and a long T-shirt so I know she's in for the night. Her dirty blonde hair hangs over her shoulders in two long pigtails.

"Hey, I tried to call you. I ordered Chinese. The leftovers are in the fridge."

"It's okay. I ate at Gabe's house." I drop my handbag next to the door. She moves over so I can plop down on the couch next to her.

"I figured. How is he doing?"

"About the same. He's sleeping a lot."

Sadness washes over me again remembering how he looked. I'm not used to seeing him like that. Pale, tired and grumpy. It's so hard to see him hurt and vulnerable. Worse, I miss him. Not in the romantic way that everyone else assumes but as my friend.

Although crying all over Zack certainly doesn't help the perception that I'm jealous.

"Maybe going over there so much isn't a good thing." Izzie says it slowly, drawing out the words. She shrugs when I look over at her. "I'm just saying."

I can't even be angry with her. She doesn't know the real reason I spend so much time at Gabe's house is so I can see his brother.

"I'm starting to think you're right. I need to get back to work. Mr. Hartwell, you remember the owner of the gallery, wants to see my next photo series as soon as it's done."

"That's great! You're really doing it, Jo. Making a living with your photography. This is awesome."

"I don't know if I'd call it making a living. But I'm so excited to have the chance to shoot what I want."

The money isn't great yet but I'm secretly thrilled. It's not easy to even have a chance at a show much less actually sell out. Now I have pretty much free license to shoot whatever I want. The proceeds from the last show will tide me over until I can figure out what I want to do. It's nice to have that freedom.

"Have you decided what you're going to work on next?" She picks up the remote and flips through the channels randomly.

"My erotic show sold out last time so I need to do something similar."

She pauses on a channel with some kind of nature program. I can tell when my words sink in because her brow furrows.

"Another erotic show?" Her giggles are infectious. "You are really trying to give your mother a heart attack!"

"What she doesn't know won't hurt her."

"Um, don't you think you should at least warn her?"

"Yes, of course. But not until I'm done. The last thing I need in my head while working on this is my mother's voice."

"Well, it's all going to hit the fan when she finds out you have another show coming up."

I acknowledge her words with a shrug. Worrying about what my mom thinks is a waste of time. "Nothing I've ever done has made her happy except for dating Gabe. Which never actually happened. The one thing she thinks I did right was a product of her imagination. That tells you everything you need to know about my relationship with my mother."

Izzie glances at me from the side of her eye. "I still think it's a tragic waste that you never got a piece of that while you could."

Her shocked outrage is still just as funny now as it was back in high school. "Iz, we were kids!"

"Whatever. Even the kid version of Gabe Marshall was some seriously prime eye-candy. You could have at least gotten naked a few times and manhandled that."

I'm laughing so hard now that she shoves me over.

"It's not funny! You know I had a serious crush on him and you just hung out with him like it was no big deal. There really weren't any secret make-out sessions that you never told me about?"

I shake my head ruefully at the wishful tone of her voice. "Sorry to disappoint you. It's never been like that with us."

"I know, I know. He's your white knight. I'm so grateful that he was there that night." She gets really quiet all of a sudden and I know she's remembering.

"It wasn't your fault, Izzie."

She manages a small smile. "Not directly but I shouldn't have left you on your own. That's part of the girlfriend code of honor."

Truthfully, she remembers more of the night in question than I do. I'd told my parents that I was sleeping over at Izzie's but we'd snuck out to go to a party at a senior's house. We'd both gotten drunk for the first time and spent the entire night giggling over the couples making out in the corners, on the steps and even right out in the open.

Then Izzie had left me on my own to go talk to Chris, the boy she'd been crushing on since she'd been transferred into AP English. Everything after that is a blur.

According to her, Gabe found me in one of the upstairs rooms fighting off three guys who wouldn't let me leave. My dress was torn and I was crying but I don't remember any of that. All I know is that he got me out of there somehow. Strangely enough, the only thing I remember is the sensation of being held close and him tapping a rhythm on my arm.

For years after that night I couldn't stand to be touched but the only thing I remember clearly is waking up in Izzie's bed the next morning.

"Well, I still say it's a shame. A man that gorgeous should never be put in the friend zone."

"He makes me feel safe," I say quietly. "I think I've been using Gabe as a crutch to keep from putting myself out there. The entire time I was dating Perry I think even he could tell something wasn't right. I stayed with him because he fit into the image my parents wanted. But he deserves better than that. And so do I."

Izzie leans over and hugs me, burying her face in my shoulder. "You deserve everything."

In that moment, I make another decision about my future. "I know what I want to do for my next project."

She looks at me askance but she got used to how I randomly change topics years ago. "Your next photo series, you mean?"

"Yes. Sensuality is always presented as the female body. Not that I don't understand why. The curves of the female form are beautiful. But I want to come at this from a different angle. I want to show the grace and sensuality in the male form."

"Do it. Maybe you'll finally stop mooning after Gabe if you find another hottie to lust after."

She rolls her eyes at my scowl. "I know. Just friends. *Whatever*. So you're focusing on the guys this time, huh?"

"That's the plan."

Her eyes sparkle as she sits up and I can tell she's warming up to the idea. "You should hire one of those sexy male models to pose for you!"

Now she's lost me. "I'm not hiring a hot guy just because you think I need to get laid. All the models for my last series were volunteers and I think it made the photos more stunning in the end because all the emotions captured were real. I was planning to do that again."

"Well, that's fine I guess as long as you find someone you actually want to see naked."

"I'm not going to do it with the guy. Besides, who says I need to do anything with anyone right now. Being a virgin isn't a crime."

"No but bypassing the extreme hotness of Gabe Marshall to date the boring guys you've been with is. No wonder you haven't given it up yet."

I have to laugh, she's so outrageous. "That has nothing to do with it."

"You need to get some girl. If you don't lose it finally you're going to start growing cobwebs all up in your lady garden. And I want more than that for you." She says this with typical Izzie aplomb, as if discussing the status of my lady parts is totally normal.

"Um, thanks for the support, I think?"

"Do you need an assistant? No matter who you end up using, you're going to need someone to rub oil on the fine, naked male specimen in question before the shoot, right?" She beams at me before getting up and bouncing into the kitchen.

"Actually, I just might." I whisper it to myself but now that the idea has been planted, it makes sense.

Isabelle for all her crazy ideas might just be onto something.

Chapter Three

Josie

Izzie drags out her laptop and convinces me to send a few emails to local talent agencies. She's way more excited about it than I am but by the time I go to my room to get ready for bed, I've started to imagine some of the shots. This is usually how it starts for me, with a vague image before I'm suddenly slammed with ideas for photos.

After washing my face and braiding my hair loosely, I change into my favorite worn T-shirt and a pair of cotton boxer shorts before climbing into bed. I plug my phone into the charger on my nightstand, ignoring the little red flag that tells me I have several missed calls. I've pushed off visiting my mom for the past week and it's time to pay the piper. I'll have to make time to see her tomorrow.

Moving out of my parents' house may have bought me some sanity but I haven't built up a backbone strong enough to break the tie completely. As much as I hate it, there's a part of me that still wants their approval. It's a dangerous cycle that keeps me chasing something that will always be just out of reach.

They weren't thrilled when I dropped out of college but I think my mother could have overlooked that if I'd had another purpose. Charity work that would raise her profile or getting married to any of the eligible bachelors she's had her eye on since we were all in nursery school together. But dropping out to focus on my art was akin to tragedy in her eyes. You'd think I'd told her I was shooting porn in my spare time.

Although in her eyes what I do is just as bad.

Thinking about my parents definitely isn't helping me relax so I roll over until I'm facing the photos on the wall next to my bed. Instantly I feel better.

The slim elegance of a woman's crossed legs. The graceful arch of a back. The passion of a couple's embrace. Every single one of these images tells a story and I'm honored to be allowed the privilege of documenting that. Even if my parents don't get it.

I fall asleep with the images in my head.

My dreams are vivid and when I wake, I feel like one big throbbing nerve ending. Maybe Izzie is right and I need to get some action before I self combust. But at least my pent up sexual frustration is good for something because by the time I get over to see Gabe again the next day, I have several pages of ideas jotted down in the little notebook I always carry around.

Sasha answers the door looking much more energetic than the last time I saw her.

"Oh my god, I'm so glad you're here." She moves back so I can come in. "He's so cranky it's unbelievable."

This isn't a surprise to me. Years of dealing with Gabe means I've seen him sick before. The man is a complete and total baby when he doesn't feel well. When he had bronchitis one year, I was worried that I was going to do him more harm than the virus.

"He's always been grumpy when he's sick."

Before I even have a chance to put my bag down, she grabs me by the hand and pulls me upstairs. I follow, trying not to trip since she isn't slowing down to give me time to catch up. When we reach Gabe's room, she shoves open the door and pulls me through behind her.

"I am going to take a walk. Maybe you can cheer him up. Nothing I've tried has worked."

Before I can even respond, she walks back out pulling the door closed behind her.

I turn to look at Gabe. "What did you do to her?"

He grunts. "I'm ready to get out of this bed."

"You look better." And he does. It's a relief actually to see him looking more like his old self.

"Better than one foot in the grave. I'm just balancing on the ledge of the grave now." He moves over slightly so I can sit beside him.

"You'd better be nice to her. She's the one preparing your food."

He cracks a smile finally. "For some reason she loves me. So I don't think she'll poison me yet."

The front door closes downstairs and then it's quiet. I don't hear anyone else moving around.

"What's been going on with you?" He shifts slightly, turning so that he can recline against his pillows but look directly at me. I can tell he's really uncomfortable and have to resist the urge to try to help him. So I rack my brain trying to think of something to talk about. Something that might distract him from how crappy he feels.

"So you know my last show sold out."

Gabe smiles. "Of course it did. It was awesome."

His unwavering support has gotten me through so many rough times in my life. It's one of the only things that I've always known that I could count on. Every time I think about telling Zack how I feel, I imagine what things would be like if it didn't work out. Then not only would I lose him but Gabe's friendship, too.

"Thank you. That means a lot. It also means that I can pretty much shoot whatever I want for my next show. Mr. Hartwell is pretty sure that he can sell whatever I give him now. So I decided to focus on the male body for my next series."

His eyes narrow. "What does that mean exactly?"

"It means that I'll be focusing on men this time around. No couples. No women. Just the male form. One male form, specifically. I think it makes sense for the whole series to be about the same person."

He shifts in the bed. "Have you already found someone?"

Suddenly, I'm not so sure I want to tell him. Sasha said that the way Zack was looking at me wasn't very brotherly but Gabe is very much the big brother type. I'm actually more worried about telling him certain things than my real big brother.

"I think I'm going to hire someone. A model."

His face goes hard immediately. "A stranger. You're going to be alone taking naked pictures of a stranger? What if the guy isn't trustworthy?"

"Don't be such a prude. We can always do a background check to make sure the guy isn't a criminal."

"You know just as well as I do that background checks aren't worth shit. I would have passed one."

I have to admit that he's right on that score. As many things as Gabe has gotten into in the past, he was usually able to charm his way out of trouble. Also, being alone with someone I don't know sounds like a bad idea. Izzie's suggestion about being my assistant doesn't sound like such a bad idea all of a sudden.

"A clean background check doesn't tell you a guy is safe. It just means he was good enough not to get caught." Gabe winces as he moves.

That's when I really look at him. This conversation is seriously stressing him out. And worrying him is the last thing I wanted to do when I came here today.

"Okay, just take it easy. I'm not doing anything yet. I'm just thinking about it."

"Promise me you won't do anything crazy. Promise me!"

"Whoa, okay. I promise. Now calm down before Sasha comes back and we're both in trouble."

Chapter Four

Zack

I haven't been able to stop thinking about the way Josie looked right before she walked away. The sight of her in tears is particularly disturbing since she rarely cries.

My distraction is particularly inconvenient right now since with Gabe out of commission I'm pulling double duty at the auto garage we co-own. It's a grind trying to keep up with the scheduled repairs and run the front desk. We have a great team of guys but most of them aren't really well-suited to customer service.

"This goddamned computer. It's broken again."

Jim, the older guy who taught both of us everything we know

about cars, swears like a drunken sailor and thinks most technology is out to get him. He was happy to take a turn standing behind the counter for any walk-ins but I've had to take time out between jobs to correct the customer information he's entered in the computer all day.

"It's okay, I've got it."

He moves away quickly, grateful to escape back to what he knows best. I type in the last information from the customer slip that he was trying to input in the system and then walk over to the front door and lock it.

Reed, one of our motorcycle specialists, is helping a customer at the other end of the counter but he can unlock the door for her when they're done. Usually I don't flip the sign to closed while there are still people in the shop but at ten minutes to seven, I've had all I can take today.

After another hour in the back finishing up, I make my escape. When I get home, I'm shocked to see Gabe sitting downstairs. He looks a little better but suddenly I'm hit with visions of him passing out and bleeding all over the floor.

"Do I even want to know how you got down here?"

He grunts. "Tired of being a fucking invalid."

There's not much I can say to that. This situation sucks no matter how you look at it. I sit next to him on the couch. "Come on. We need to get you back in bed."

"I was waiting for you for a reason. It's about Josie. She's decided on the subject of her next photo series."

I shift uncomfortably in my seat. We went to her first gallery show a few weeks ago and I was blown away. Gabe had told me that she was taking erotic pictures but I hadn't been prepared for how intense the photos were. They weren't so much about sex as they were about vulnerability. Fear. Longing. Looking at her photos was like taking a peek into her most private thoughts and the experience left me completely gutted.

I want to support her but I'm not sure how much I can take. Standing in a gallery while random people looked at her work felt like letting others see her naked.

God help me if she ever decides to do a self-portrait.

"Another show like last time? I'm sure her parents are thrilled."

"No. Something different." His voice is rising as he speaks and I can tell how agitated he is. "She says she wants to focus on the male body. I already told her *no fucking way*."

Suddenly my skin feels too tight. All I can see is Josie taking pictures of some guy, talking to him, touching him and it's killing me. But after my initial surge of rage and jealousy then I circle around right back to where I'm sitting. On a couch with the only person Josie really wants.

"Gabe, she's a big girl. If she wants to take nude pictures, you can't stop her."

Not to mention that he has a girlfriend. It drives me crazy that he still has this weird sense of ownership over Josie, like she belongs to him. I stand and he struggles to his feet as well. I immediately put my arm around his waist, holding him against me as we walk.

He grunts in pain as we ascend the stairs. "The crazy woman is thinking about hiring some random guy to get naked for her. You really want her spending hours at a time with some naked dude? What if this guy hurts her?"

His words are like being dunked in ice water. Josie alone at the mercy of some guy? Oh *hell no*. Every muscle in my body tenses simultaneously and Gabe immediately tunes in to my distress.

"Yeah, that's what I thought. You don't like the idea any more than I do. You have to stop her, Zack."

It's so incredibly ironic that he's passing the responsibility off to me when he's the one that Josie would do anything for.

"How the hell am I supposed to do that? You're the one she listens to, not me."

"Talk to her, please."

By this time we've reached his room and Gabe looks absolutely destroyed by the effort it took to climb the stairs. As much as I want to wash my hands of this entire situation, I can't. Because if I don't agree, he'll wear himself down trying to handle it. He's in no condition to deal with this right now. Once again I find myself in an impossible position, held hostage by my love for the both of them.

"Okay, I'll talk to her. But you know it's impossible to make Josie see reason when she's got her mind set on something."

"Just try." Gabe sinks down slowly onto the bed and lets out a ragged sigh of relief as he collapses against the pillows. "You're the only one I trust to take care of her. Jo is special, you know she is. I just need her to be safe."

"I've got it, bro."

His eyes are already closed and I doubt he heard me but there's a sense of peace on his features. Gabe and I have always had each other's back so he's counting on me to fix this since he can't.

———

*B*y the next day I've worked myself up to go see Josie. Gabe has asked me to talk to her as if that's an easy thing. But Josephine Harlow is notoriously stubborn. I'm already anticipating that I'll be leaving with claw marks after our conversation. Want to know the really sick thing?

I'm actually looking forward to it.

How pathetic is it that my twisted heart is happy with any scrap of her attention, even the negative kind?

Just the thought puts me further into my cranky mood.

When I reach the stately white Victorian home that she's recently moved to, I park on the street right in front of the house. As I get out, I look around curiously, taking in the well-manicured lawns and expensive cars in the drives of most of the other homes. Fancy.

I should have expected this since Jo's parents live in the kind of hoity toity community where everyone looks like a plastic doll. I would have thought that her new neighborhood would be different since she's been so determined to get away from that world. Then I remember that she lives with her friend Isabelle. I've met Isabelle a few times but my mind brings forth only a vague recollection of a gangly girl with long blond hair and braces.

I didn't think I looked that bad but an older man getting out of his car a few houses over stares at me openly as I walk up the drive to the house. I guess bad is relative. Where I'm from I wouldn't get a second glance but in this neighborhood, I look like a walking felony. My dark hair is gelled up into spikes today and the sleeveless black shirt I'm wearing exposes all the tattoos on my arms. No doubt I'll give her neighbors something to gossip about over their dinner tables tonight.

Just before the gawking grandpa reaches his front door, I raise my hand and wave gaily. "Nice day, isn't it?"

He looks petrified and then rushes inside his house. The door slams behind him.

"Well, I hope it wasn't something I said."

Just when I'm about to knock on Josie's door, it opens and a young blond guy walks out, muttering an apology as he passes. I turn around and another guy appears in the doorway.

This one looks me up and down and then says, "You're probably out of luck, man. The call sheet specifically said they wanted late twenties."

"Excuse me?"

He shrugs. "Just trying to help you out. You've got a baby face. But if you think you can fool them, go for it."

By the time I've worked out what he said, he's gone. I watch wordlessly as he walks down the drive and gets in a car parked across the street. The front door is still hanging open so I push it open all the way and step inside. Closing it behind me, I follow the sound of voices and laughter.

If Josie is having a party then I've officially bought myself some more time. I'm not looking forward to trying to talk her out of this crazy idea. But nothing prepares me for what I see when I enter the living room.

Josie sits behind a white folding table chewing absently on the end of a pencil. A blonde that I immediately recognize as Isabelle stands right behind her. She's filled out some and her hair is slightly darker but it's definitely her. They both stare mesmerized at the guy undressing in the middle of the room.

The guy they're watching is bare chested and doing something with his abs that makes them look like they're rippling. When he goes to unbutton his jeans, I jerk my gaze away, trying to look at something, *anything*, other than this dude's junk. That's when I notice the others.

My mouth falls open.

There's an entire line of shirtless young guys waiting their turn to approach the table.

"What the hell is going on here?"

My voice breaks through the noise in the room and everyone turns to look at me simultaneously. The dude undulating his abs pauses mid-ripple. Isabelle is having a really hard time deciding whether she wants to look at that or me.

Josie stands, her chair making a loud screeching sound as she pushes away from the table. "Zack? What are you doing here?"

I gesture around me. "I'm here to talk to you. Gabe told me what you're up to but he didn't mention that you'd already started hiring."

Her eyes skitter away. "He doesn't know."

"I guessed that part. I'm guessing he also doesn't know that you're holding auditions for Magic Mike in your living room?"

She glances behind her sheepishly at the guy with the abs who is watching us with confusion. He points at his pants.

"Should I take these off? Because I can do this thing with my thigh muscles that you should see."

Isabelle nods her head. "We should *definitely* see that."

All at once, I can't take any more. "No, we don't need to see that. Get your shit and get out. All of you. Out!"

The guy looks like he wants to say something but when I turn to him, the glower on my face must convince him that it's not worth it. He grabs his shirt from the floor and pulls it over his head.

Isabelle rushes forward. "Please leave your cards, gentlemen. We'll call you when we've made a decision."

The other guys standing in line grumble as they file out of the room toward the front door. A few are taking longer than necessary so I clap my hands. "Let's go!"

Josie looks appalled. She stomps over and grabs my arm. "You have some nerve. Who the hell do you think you are?"

Is she fucking kidding me? We face each other in a standoff. Josie raises an eyebrow when I don't answer right away. My annoyance fades a little as I watch her get more and more pissed off. It doesn't help that she's hot when she's all worked up like this. She looks like she'll bite my face off if I get too close.

"I'm the guy who just cleared all the potential serial killers out of your living room. *You're welcome.*"

"I'm not an idiot, Zack. We didn't just grab random guys off the street. We got these candidates from a reputable modeling agency. How am I supposed to explain what just happened?"

"I don't care how the hell you explain it. But I wasn't about to stand there and let that guy take his pants off."

Suddenly she clamps her hand over her mouth. My stomach clenches, worried that she'll start crying. But a soft giggle escapes from behind her fingers.

"Don't you dare laugh."

Finally she seems to get herself under control. "What else can I do? I have to laugh or I'll scream instead. Thanks to you, this entire day has been a waste of time. After that fiasco the agency isn't going to send me any other models and I don't really want to start over with another agency."

She walks over to the couch and sinks down. Her shoulders slump forward and she lets out a long sigh. I kneel on the floor in front of her and when she meets my eyes, all the fight drains out of me. It's not like her to look so dejected. So defeated.

"Why is this so important, Jo? What's the rush?"

"Time is counting down until my next show and I've got nothing. The owner of the gallery has been really patient and supportive but if I don't deliver, then he's not going to wait forever."

Now I feel guilty. Even though my intention was to get her to change her mind, it hadn't fully hit me that she's doing this to further her photography career. Her last show was phenomenal and it makes total sense that she would feel pressure to top that.

Maybe that's what makes the craziest thing ever pop out of my mouth next.

"Use me."

Josie looks just as shocked as I feel. For several moments neither of us moves, frozen into awkwardness before she lets out a startled laugh.

"That's ridiculous."

Even though I feel the same, hearing her say it kind of pisses me off. Thigh ripple guy is a candidate but not me?

"Why is that so ridiculous? You need a naked guy. I'm a guy. Why can't you use me?"

"Because you're *you*," she says as if that makes total sense. "I can't... we can't... there's just no way that would work." She jumps up and starts gathering all the papers on the table into a pile. She drags the chair back into the kitchen while I trail behind her.

"Why not? You don't think I'm pinup material?" I already know that I'm not Josie's dream man. Her type is tall, dark and handsome. Not tall, snarky and inked. But it's fun to fuck with her anyway.

She blushes and swipes a stray piece of hair behind her ear. Her eyes are everywhere but on me.

"It's not that. But modeling isn't something you just jump into. You have to be really comfortable in your skin and very aware of your body and how it moves."

"Are you really going to pretend that's why you had those guys taking their shirts off? To make sure they're comfortable in their skin? It had nothing to do with wanting to see them naked, huh?"

She shrugs. "If I'm going to focus on the sensuality of the male body, it makes sense to find one that most women would find attractive. It might seem shallow but then again sexuality isn't an equal opportunity game. Physical attraction is a huge part of it. Plus, if they can't even take their shirt off then they won't be able to handle posing completely nude."

Her voice lowers and one of her hands lands on her neck. It hits me then how intimate this conversation is and how close we're standing.

"I've never had a problem with nudity." I grip the back of my shirt and pull it over my head.

Josie's mouth opens and closes a few times. Her eyes roam over my exposed chest. "I see that."

"Unless you have a problem with all the ink."

At my words, her eyes drop to the tattoos on my chest. I have a massive phoenix on my left pec whose head rests on my shoulder while the body covers my ribs. The feet go below the waistband of my jeans. There are several lines of poetry on my right ribs and my moms' names running around my left bicep. I also have full sleeves of ink covering both forearms. It's a lot to look at but she doesn't seem put off by it at all. Her eyes soften as she takes it all in.

Stunned, I look into her eyes for the first time in… well, ever. Her cheeks are flushed, her dark eyes bright and that lush bottom lip keeps finding its way between her teeth. On another woman these same signs would equal arousal. Desire. But this is Jo and I've never seen her look at me like this before. Which makes me wonder if the sudden sexual awareness I feel around her is a mutual thing.

Do I even want it to be?

Isabelle comes back in then and skids to a halt in the doorway. The tension between us is palpable and she looks like she wants to turn around and run back out. She glances between us hesitantly. "I just remembered that I have that thing. So, I'm going to go."

"What thing?" Josie demands.

She pulls her eyes away from my chest and looks over at her friend. She's making a face that I can tell means she doesn't want Isabelle to leave her alone with me.

"You know, the thing with that guy. I'll tell you about it later." Isabelle's eyes dart over to me and then she looks me over from head to toe. "Much later. Bye!"

Josie shakes her head as Isabelle practically runs out of the room. "Wow. All my friends are traitors today."

"Your friends care about you. And Isabelle knows that you're safe with me."

"Am I?" After glancing at my chest a few more times, she turns around and walks back to the table. She picks up one of the forms on the stack and then holds it out to me.

"What's that?"

"It's an application. If you're going to do this, then you'll need to sign the photo release form. Unless you're backing out?" She raises an eyebrow.

I can tell from the way she's not meeting my eyes that she's hoping I will. That makes me all the more determined to do this. I grab the form and pick up one of the pens on the table.

"Not a chance."

Chapter Five

Zack

I sign the form without even reading it. I doubt Josie is angling to take advantage of me. I glance up and when our eyes meet, she quickly looks away. Oh yeah, she's hoping I chicken out so she can go back to interviewing Chippendale dancers. Well, she's stuck with me for now.

I hand her the form. "Done. I guess this means I can't sue you for sexual harassment."

Her smile appears and disappears so quickly I almost miss it. Damn, it's fun to rile her. But I guess we should call a truce if she's going to be taking pictures of me naked. Having pictures of my junk out there for the world to see doesn't really bother me that much. I don't give a fuck what anyone thinks. But she could make me look really bad.

Or really *small*.

Suddenly I'm not so sure about this. I probably should have asked a few questions before signing up to be her guinea pig.

"Am I allowed to ask questions about your show? How naked are we really getting with this?"

She rolls her eyes and points me to the couch. Since she hasn't answered me, I guess that's a no to the asking questions thing. I wait patiently while she does complicated shit to her camera and then starts snapping pictures.

"Should I just take the rest of my clothes off now? How are we doing this?"

I'm charmed by the blush that works up from her neck and spreads to her cheeks. She's trying so hard to act nonchalant but that's impossible when you've known someone as long as I've known Josie. Rough language and raunchy jokes have always made her blush.

"Not yet. I need to get a feel for how you move first. These are just test shots."

"Why not just get to it?"

I see a brief flash of her smile before she disappears behind the camera again. The shutter clicks as she moves around me.

"Foreplay, Zachary. It's a thing for a reason."

"Believe me, I know. But it's usually a lot more pleasurable than this."

This is weird, feeling like I'm on display. Even though it's what I signed up for, since I can't see her face it feels like I'm doing this with a stranger.

"Can you at least tell me what your show is about? Or is it just about dongs in general?"

She lowers the camera. "Real mature."

"Well, you haven't told me anything. What am I supposed to think?"

She considers this and then shrugs. "Erotic art usually focuses on the female form. I want to explore sensuality from the opposite view."

It sounds like bullshit to me but I don't say anything. If she wants an excuse to photograph naked dudes that's fine but why do women always have to make everything so complicated? Men don't try to dress up our desires. We want to see naked women because we like seeing naked women. End of story.

Something in my face must give away my true feelings because she suddenly lowers the camera again.

"What? Just say whatever it is you're thinking. You don't think that men can be sex objects?" Her nose crinkles derisively.

"Sure. I think most men think of themselves that way. But that still doesn't answer my question. I want to know what's in it for *you*. Why this specifically and not something else?"

"I've decided to go after the things I want this year. To be brave and confident. Playing it safe is boring. I'm going to do the unexpected from now. Have some adventures."

I move around, trying to get comfortable and she motions with her hand for me to go the other way. Then she puts the camera down.

"Let's try something different."

She drags the pillows off the couch and to the floor. "Sit here. Like you're just hanging out."

I sit on the first cushion with my back resting against the couch. There's nothing special about the way I'm posed, lounging with one knee propped up, but she makes a soft sound of happiness. Almost like she's humming. That's all it takes. With that one careless sound my dick is ready for action.

Shit.

My sudden attraction for Josie is extremely inconvenient. I shift around, hoping that my jeans conceal the fact that I'm hard as a rock. But Josie doesn't seem to notice. In fact, she seems happy, moving around me clicking away. My heart stutters a little when one side of her mouth lifts slightly into that sexy little smirk she does. Instinctively, I smile back.

She lowers the camera. Our eyes meet.

Something changes in that moment and suddenly things are different. I'm acutely aware of every sensation, including the hard edge of the couch behind me and the rough material of my jeans rubbing against my erection. Even my skin feels uncomfortably tight all of a sudden. When I look back at Josie, she bites her lip and looks away.

"Why did you really stop the auditions, Zack?"

"I had to."

"Why? I mean, why do you even care?"

What a loaded fucking question.

Because I don't want naked guys around her. Because I worry about her. Because I want to be the one she needs. But I can't say any of that so I go with the truth because it's simpler. And just as loaded.

"Gabe asked me to."

And there we have it. The thing that will always be between us.

Josie rolls her eyes. "Unbelievable. I'm not completely reckless, you know. That's why we did the auditions as a group. For safety. Izzie has also offered to be there while I shoot so I'm not alone with anyone. Gabe worries too much."

"Right."

Her fingers tighten around the camera. "Is there something else you want to say?"

"Just wondering if there's an ulterior motive to this whole thing. You know that Gabe worries about you. And you knew that doing this would drive him insane."

Her eyes flash. "What are you trying to say? That I did this to get his attention?"

That's exactly what I'm saying but I can tell that I've just opened up a minefield. She's always been touchy when I point out her crush on Gabe. That's part of what made it so much fun to annoy her. At least it was fun until I realized that I'd give anything to be the one she noticed. Not so much fun then.

When I don't say anything else she closes her eyes and that's how I know she's *really* mad.

"I swear if I hadn't known you so long Zack Marshall I would never speak to you again. Here's a newsflash. *Everything isn't about Gabe.*"

That's just it though. It always has been before. A fact that I long ago learned to live with.

"You want me to believe this isn't about him, then help me understand."

She turns and walks away. I sag back against the couch. We've always pestered each other but this is different. Her anger is a palpable thing and I'm starting to realize that I might have pushed her too far.

Just when I'm contemplating whether I should go after her and apologize, she comes back. As she walks she juggles one of those huge photo albums, the kind my mom has all of our baby pictures in. Finally she pulls out a photo and hands it to me.

The couple in the picture are wrapped around each other without anything between them. They're looking deeply into each other's eyes while making love. The camera's angle makes it look like I'm right there in the bed with them.

Like all of Josie's pictures it makes me uncomfortable and excited and ... surprisingly envious.

"This wasn't in your show," I say finally.

"No. It was too explicit for the show but I had to capture the moment."

Her finger trails over the image and I shudder as if she's touched me.

"It's beautiful, Josie." It's completely inadequate as far as description goes but true nonetheless.

"The picture is technically beautiful, yes. But that's not why I kept this shot. Look at how he's looking at her." Her eyes drop to the image again and I can't miss the wistful tone of her voice.

It's what I see in her face that makes me look again, trying to see what she sees. Trying to feel what she feels. I want so badly to understand what drives her. To get even a little insight into what makes her happy.

"They look like they're really in love."

"That's because they are. When I was photographing them, even though I was there taking pictures, for them it was like they were alone. Nothing could intrude on the world they created together. It was fascinating to me."

Her words weave a spell until I'm as caught up as the people in the picture. It feels like we're in our own little world now as she's talking and I can't imagine being anywhere else.

"I want to understand why people are willing to throw away everything for passion. *Wars have been fought for this.* My art is the only place that I can learn, grow and explore without other people's judgments in the way. How else can I understand what I've never experienced?"

I'm so enthralled with her, completely mesmerized by the sound of her voice, that the meaning of her words almost don't register. When they do, my heart starts a wild thump behind my rib cage. Does that mean what I think it means? I almost can't breathe, the need to find out is so overwhelming.

"What do you mean never experienced?"

My question breaks the tranquil mood around us and her face immediately closes up. She blinks several times and then sits back to put some space between us. "Nothing. Forget I said anything."

"The hell I'll forget it."

She shrinks back but this time I follow. Since she's sitting with her back against the couch, there's nowhere for her to go when I put my arm down blocking her in. "All those times with Gabe..."

"All those times were just two friends hanging out. I've told you that before." Even though she looks cornered, her chin lifts defiantly. Like she's daring me to contradict her.

"You have to understand how hard that is to believe. It's been years. *Years*. You've been a part of our lives for so long. In the beginning I figured you were just attached to Gabe because he saved you. But you just kept showing up."

Josie's hand comes up and settles on my cheek. The entire world could stop spinning in this moment and I wouldn't know.

"He's not the one I showed up for," she whispers.

Then she's kissing me and all the thoughts in my head disintegrate and my entire being centers on the place where we connect. Her lips are warm and she's so soft and perfect and in that moment, nothing else matters.

Her mouth opens and her tongue strokes against mine and suddenly I understand all that shit she was saying before. I understand why people would throw away anything for a moment of passion. I understand why wars are fought for this.

Because I'd fight anything to keep her right where she is.

Chapter Six

Josie

When we finally break the kiss we're both breathing hard and Zack looks shaky and slightly frightened. I'm sure I look the same way because it's how I feel. Disoriented and scared as hell because I didn't know that it could be like that.

I didn't know that a kiss could shake up your entire world.

"Josie," he whispers.

I feel the sound of my name against my lips and something clenches hard in my lower belly. Then he's kissing me again, harder, deeper this time. He's been passive up until now but his arm curls under me holding me against him. My chest plasters to his and I absolutely melt as every part of me merges into every part of him. My nipples brush against his chest and they're suddenly so hard it's painful. The ache between my thighs is worse now and as if he knows, his palm flattens on my lower back urging me to straddle him.

When I do, he lets out a deep, needy sound that I'll never forget.

Until he pulls back, his face tortured. "What are we doing?"

"Kissing." I can't seem to keep my hands away from his chest. I want to touch him all over.

He grabs my hands and holds them still as we pant, our breath mingling together. "This is crazy. This is not why I came over here."

"I know."

"And I would never take advantage of you."

"*I know.* Why would you think you're taking advantage? I want you. You want me."

When he doesn't say anything, I pull back a bit so I can see his face. What I see makes my heart sink. He looks cornered.

"At least I thought you wanted me."

I shift back slightly so I'm not rubbing right up against the hard length in his jeans. "I can feel that you want me."

"There's more to this than just the heat of the moment."

Now that pisses me off. He can't deny that he wants me physically but to act like what just happened is a purely chemical thing is a slap in the face.

"So I could have been any willing woman and you would have reacted the same way. Good to know."

He sighs. "That's not what I meant. I just think a lot of things have happened lately. Anyone would be confused. I don't want to take advantage of that."

"I'm not the one who's confused. The past few weeks have been a revelation for me. I don't want to waste any more time. I'm going after the things I want. The things that make me happy. This isn't a new thing for me, Zack. Feeling this way. And I don't think it is for you either. You've never thought of me like this before today?"

"Of course. You're beautiful, Josie."

"Don't give me that." Frustration makes my voice sharper than I intend. "The 'you're beautiful' thing. That's what you say to your little cousin when she's dressed up for prom. Tell me you've never thought of me *like this*."

I point to the picture on the floor between us.

"Fuck." The word seems to escape before he can stop it. "*Of course I have.* Look at you." His eyes roam over me from the gap in my shirt to my long hair which I know has to look pretty wild after he's had his hands in it.

"Yes, Zack. Look at me."

I place my hands on his cheeks and rest my forehead against his. We sit like that breathing the same air for a minute before I kiss him again. He doesn't move but our lips cling like they don't want to separate any more than I do. He's so rigid beneath me, like he's afraid to make any moves or I'll break.

Finally he meets my eyes. "I'm trying to do the right thing here, Jo."

I push away and climb off his lap. My fingers fumble the buttons as I attempt to cover my cleavage. His eyes follow the movement. Even while he's claiming to want to protect me, he can't keep his eyes off my breasts.

"This is a lot to take in. I don't want us to do something we'll regret. You'd hate me, Jo and I couldn't take that. You can have any guy that you want."

"Don't do that. I can take almost anything from you but sympathy."

It's a pain unlike anything I've ever felt to watch him try to backpedal his way out of this. My worst nightmare has come true. I told Zack how I feel and he doesn't want me.

"It's not like that, Josie—"

"Just go home, Zack. If you value our friendship at all, just leave me alone."

———

I watch silently as Zack yanks his shirt over his head and then walks away. When the front door slams behind him a wave of emotion passes through me that's so potent I almost can't breathe.

Tears aren't my usual response to confrontation so I'm ashamed at the tears that spill down my cheeks. If it was anyone else I would be on my feet and spouting curse words.

But this is Zack.

To hear such ugly accusations coming from him tore me up inside. Maybe that's what hurts the most, that one of my closest friends could have such a low opinion of me. He really thinks that everything I'm doing is part of some diabolical plan to get Gabe's attention. How could he really think that I'd try to break up his brother's relationship? Not only because it's untrue but because it's so unlike me. He knows me and that I'd never do something like that.

At least I thought he did.

I'm not sure how long I'm sitting there before the door opens again. I sit up, ready to do battle when Isabelle turns the corner. She looks at me on the couch and then glances around the room.

"Where is he?"

"Who?" I get up and walk into the kitchen. I take down a mug and start water boiling for tea. Isabelle follows behind me and I know she's waiting to get the scoop but I can't look at her. She always sees everything and I'm not ready to talk about this yet.

"Zack. The tattooed temptation. I tried to give you guys some time alone but I have book club tonight so I need to get ready."

"You didn't need to do that. He had to get home."

She pulls down another mug and then digs in the pantry for the tea. When she emerges, she's got the Earl Grey blend that she favors and the raspberry green tea for me.

"I cannot believe I never realized how hot he is. Back in high school he seemed so aloof and I don't know, above it all. Like he didn't really care about anything. I never would have guessed he had *that* hiding under his clothes." She fans her face dramatically. When I shrug but don't say anything, she narrows her eyes. "But you didn't seem so surprised by it."

"Oh I was surprised. Totally surprised."

Which is not an exaggeration at all. As many times as I've dreamed of Zack, the reality is so much better than my imagination. I can't hold back a little sigh remembering the lean muscles in his chest, leading into his jeans. All the designs on his pecs, especially the one that extends down over his ribs only added to the hotness.

Now I'm not going to just be dreaming about him naked but I'll be imagining myself tracing the lines of that tattoo. Of having the right to memorize every detail of it. Those dreams will hurt all the more now that I know what I'm missing. Just his kiss has ruined me.

When I got up this morning I was so sure of what I wanted and how to get there. Taking control of my life seemed like an easier plan before I was confronted with Zack in the flesh. It's a lot easier to decide to move on when I'm not staring at everything I've ever wanted.

Izzie covers her mouth with her hand. "Oh my god."

"What?"

"All this time, you've been telling the truth?"

"What do you mean?"

She's staring at me with a strange expression on her face. It makes me uncomfortable, so I focus on putting sugar in my tea. When I look up again, she's still watching me but the expression on her face has shifted from shock to... pity?

"You kept insisting there was nothing between you and Gabe. Of course, I thought you were just saying that because it was so obvious that you were in love. But now I see what's really going on. You're in love but not with him. It's Zack. He's the one."

All I can do is nod, my throat suddenly so thick that I can barely swallow. Izzie follows as I carry my tea to the couch. I place it carefully on the side table and then curl up against the cushions, dragging a nubby throw blanket around my legs. Ever since Zack left, it's like I have this chill I can't shake.

"It's always been him. But he doesn't feel the same way so it doesn't matter."

"Are you sure? The way he was looking at you earlier almost made my panties melt. How could I have missed this?"

I can't help but laugh at her disgruntled question. "I've gotten pretty good at hiding how I feel. There was no use in broadcasting it around. He's not mine and never will be. Even if he likes how I look, his relationship with his brother comes first. He only sees me as 'Gabe's girl' and I don't see that changing any time soon."

After our argument earlier, this point is especially obvious. I scoot down on the couch and rest my head on Izzie's shoulder.

"Do you want me to stay home tonight?"

Izzie's book club is really more like a happy hour club. Several girls in her English lit class last year proposed meeting at a local restaurant to talk about what they've been reading instead of doing it at their houses. But they spend the majority of the time getting drunk instead of talking about the book. Which Izzie has pointed out explains why their book club has been going strong for the past year instead of fizzling out like the other ones she's belonged to over the years.

"No, don't do that. Plus, I'm supposed to go see my mom this afternoon anyway. I've been putting it off for the past few days and you know how she gets when she decides I'm ignoring her."

Izzie rests her head on top of mine. "I know. Well, it could be worse. She could decide to drop by here. Remember when you first moved in?"

"Don't speak of it. I swear if you say her name three times she might appear."

We laugh together and Izzie starts talking about the guys she got cards from earlier. Normally Izzie takes hours getting ready to go out but I can tell she's hanging around so I don't have to be alone. It makes me feel better having her there and her warm presence helps plug a few of the gaping holes in my heart.

———

When I pull up in my parents' driveway a few hours later, I silently count to ten before I get out of the car. I give myself a mental pep talk as I walk up the carefully edged walkway and then open the door with my key. Visiting my mother is like taking off a bandage.

It's going to hurt either way so it's best done without lingering too long beforehand.

She's in the parlor having tea just like every other day at four o'clock. Growing up, this was my favorite room in the house. I used to call it the "blue room". The delicate Queen Anne style chairs seemed like they were fit for a princess and I always felt special when I was allowed to sit with mother while she had tea. Sometimes if she was distracted, she'd forget I was here and I would watch her write letters at the Chippendale desk in the corner. My mother has never been a particularly demonstrative woman and spending that time with her made me feel close to her.

As I got older tea time lost it's magic as it became just another opportunity for my mother to list all the ways I've disappointed her over the years but I still love this room. It's one of the only things that makes these weekly visits tolerable.

"Hello mother. You're looking well."

She tilts her head slightly so I can kiss her cheek. Her dark hair is twisted up into an elegant chignon and the dark green sheath dress she's wearing complements her favorite pearls perfectly. I don't recognize it so it must be new. I take my seat and watch while she pours the tea. I haven't even added sugar before she starts.

"You're late, Josephine." Her lips form a slight moue of distress. She must really be upset today. Usually she doesn't like to make facial expressions anymore. It might cost her another unit of Botox.

I instantly feel guilty for the uncharitable thought. I know better than anyone what it's like to live amongst people who value women only for what they look like instead of what they think or feel or do. My mother has been a product of that environment a lot longer than I have. I'm sure it's diffi-cult to live that way.

"Sorry. I've been busy lately."

"What's so important that you can't visit your mother?"

I sigh. Here we go. "You know that Gabe hasn't been well. I've been spending time at his house, helping out wherever I can."

"Oh, well. That's understandable. The two of you have always made a striking couple. Taking care of him when he needs you will hopefully make him see what's right in front of his face. Especially since you blew things with Perry."

"I didn't blow things with Perry. I broke up with him. I didn't love him. And Gabe and I are just friends." I don't bother telling her again that we've never been anything more than that. I've been saying it for years and I think she's determined to ignore anything that doesn't fit the vision in her head.

"So? You have shared history. That's an advantage. You need to get him off the market and fast. He's wealthy and handsome. His family is a concern of course but I suppose you can't have everything."

I ignore the subtle dig because I've promised myself that I won't let her get to me. But hearing anyone put down Paula and Debbie makes me so angry. They've been like my fairy godmothers in so many ways, a fact that annoys my mother greatly.

"He has a girlfriend."

"When has that ever stopped anyone? Things are cutthroat these days and you need to find someone who won't mind your eccentricities."

"You mean my art?"

"Don't start Josephine. You know how we feel about you taking those pornographic pictures!"

"Mom! You promised."

Her hand flutters to her throat. "I know and I'm trying to be supportive but darling, really? Cass Michaelson was at that exhibit and I had to listen to her snide comments at garden club for three weeks straight. She kept talking about how she used to model and asking if you do portraits on commission. As if you'd want to take her picture anyway."

"What's wrong with that? Maybe she was trying to be nice."

"Hah! She used to model for one of those filthy skin mags. What if people think that's what you do?"

It takes all my willpower to keep my eyes from rolling out of my head. "I doubt anyone else cares, Mom."

"Your father is thinking about running for state's attorney next year and we don't need any more skeletons to deal with after your brother's episode last year."

Her casual mention of my brother sends my breath from my chest. My hand shakes as I set my teacup down on the tray. My older brother, James, has always gone overboard to win our parents approval. For years he succeeded, graduating at the top of his class at Georgetown University before entering Yale Law.

After that he moved to New York and worked for one of the top firms in the country. He was on the fast track to partnership until he had a breakdown from all the pressure. He was found wandering around his neighborhood in his robe and slippers in the early morning by the police.

The fact that my parents consider him an embarrassment is so heartless. He's always done everything he could to be the perfect son and his desire to please them is ultimately what drove him past the breaking point.

"Okay, I have to go."

I ignore her usual litany of complaints and kiss her cheek briefly before I head upstairs. My father is in his study just as I knew he would be. His desk is covered in documents and his lips move slightly as he reads. He looks up when I come in.

"Hey pumpkin. When did you get here?"

"About ten minutes ago. I wanted to say hi before I left. What are you working on?"

"Just a new case. Busy, busy. Tell me, how is Isabelle?"

"She's great. Still in school, working toward her degree in library science."

"Excellent. She always did love her books."

He's already spacing out, his eyes darting back to his computer screen. My heart sinks a little but this is the way of my world. One parent who's way too interested and one who isn't interested at all.

"I'll leave you to it, then." I kiss the top of his head and pull the study door closed behind me. When I turn around, I'm yanked off my feet and twirled around.

"What the–"

When I see who it is, I let out a squeal. "Jamie! You're here!" I grab him around the waist in a bear hug. "You sneak! I had no idea you were coming into town."

"It was a spur of the moment thing."

Now that I'm looking at him, I can see the lines around his eyes are more pronounced than usual and there's a haunted look in his eyes that wasn't there before. My brother looks like he's been through some things since I saw him last.

"How long are you staying?"

"Actually I took a leave of absence. I needed one."

He throws an arm around my neck as we walk back down the hall. Growing up, we weren't as close as I'd have liked just due to the age gap. But once I was a teenager, the five years between us didn't seem quite so great. Jamie always understood when I complained about mom setting me up with yet another eligible bachelor or belittling the things I care about. He understands better than anyone how parental pressure can drive you crazy.

"So where are you staying? Not here?"

He cringes. "I didn't really think that part through. I haven't even been here an hour and Dad already asked if I would be working with him at the firm. I shouldn't say asked. *Assumed*. I don't think a leave of absence is a thing he understands."

I pull out my phone and text Izzie.

- - Okay if Jamie crashes in the guest room while he's in town?

She replies back immediately.

- - Of course! Haven't seen him in ages. C u soon <3

I turn around and drag Jamie back to his room. "Grab your stuff and come with me."

"Where are we going?" He looks amused but follows my directions, grabbing a black duffel from the bed.

"I'm rooming with Isabelle now and she said it's cool if you crash with us for a while. There's no way I'm leaving you here."

"You've certainly changed. What happened to the girl who was so worried about what everyone thinks?"

"She finally learned that *everyone* is never satisfied. I'd rather look back and regret the things I did than the things I never had the courage to try. From now on I'm living life full throttle. And so are you."

He follows me down the stairs and as we pass by, my mother stares at us both in shock. Her voice calls out behind us but we don't stop.

As we cross the threshold into the frigid evening air, it feels like we're breaking free.

Chapter Seven

Zack

I'll always consider it a miracle that I managed to get home without getting into an accident. My focus is a source of pride but today... I'm running on fumes. The entire drive my mind tortures me with possibilities. Josie being untouched. Josie being in love with me.

Josie being mine.

Once I'm home, I pace downstairs unsure of what my next move should be. If Gabe was never with Josie then I have to rewrite the events of the last five or so years. I have to acknowledge that everything I thought I knew has just been torn apart.

I don't know what to believe and I'm reluctant to ask the only other person involved.

Before I can talk myself out of it, I bound up the stairs and knock on his door. At the sound of his call, I open it. He's propped up against his pillows reading a book. I notice with relief that Sasha isn't around. I'm not sure I can have this conversation with an audience.

Gabe takes one look at me and chuckles. "Josie must have been pissed."

For a moment, I panic. How did he know where I was? Going to see Josie today was a spur of the moment thing. The mirror over his dresser reflects my image back to me and I look myself over quickly. My shirt looks a little rumpled but otherwise, I look like I normally do.

Do I have lipstick on my face or something? Although that doesn't make sense because Jo doesn't even wear lipstick. Not that I've ever seen anyway.

"Am I wearing a sign? How did you know I saw Jo?"

He tosses his book on the nightstand next to the bed. "You look like you've just gone three rounds with a champ. So what did she say?"

I sit on the edge of his bed. "The crazy woman was actually auditioning half naked guys right in her living room."

Gabe laughs. "I'm sure that was Izzie's idea."

I grunt, not seeing the humor at all. "They were from some agency she called. Whatever the case, I told them all to get the hell out."

"I bet she loved that."

An image of Josie writhing on my lap derails my thoughts. Then the look on her face when she said I was the reason she's been here all along. How could I have missed something so huge? It's like thinking everything is a blur your entire life only to put on glasses for the first time.

I can feel Gabe watching me, waiting for me to continue the story.

"Can I ask you something?"

"Sure."

"Josie mentioned something today." I halt, not even sure how to proceed. We've had this conversation before and Gabe has always said that they were just friends but I took it as him saying that they didn't have a relationship *right then*. Not that they had *never* had one.

"I think she's a virgin," I blurt out.

Gabe clasps his hands in front of him on top of the covers. "Why would you think that? She was dating Perry for a long time. And she's had other boyfriends before."

"Just something she said. But I figured that couldn't be true anyway, right?"

He finally realizes what I'm getting at. "Well, I wouldn't know either way. I wasn't her first, if that's what you're asking."

"You were never with Josie. *Ever?*"

He shakes his head.

My breath leaves my body in a huff of surprise. He's told me this before but I didn't believe him then. Part of me is scared to believe it now. Because if it's true then I've wasted years ignoring the way I feel about her. Years of pushing away the one woman I want to get close to.

"Zack. Zack?"

I must look pretty crazy because Gabe is watching me with open concern.

"Hey, I know she probably gave you hell but it'll be fine. You stopped her from making a huge mistake and once she calms down she'll see that. Give it a few days and things will be back to usual."

Usual. Right.

That word means something entirely different now. The usual is that while I've been lusting after Josie, she's been feeling the same way. The usual is that Josie is a twenty-one-year-old virgin and she's obviously looking to change that fact. To the point where she's willing to hire some random guy to do it.

I don't want things to go back to usual.

If Josie wants me to notice her, mission accomplished. And if she's looking to understand passion, then I'm the one to show her. There's no doubt in my mind about that.

Gabe takes my facial expression as worry rather than resolve. "Seriously, don't look so worried. It's Josie. She's mad right now but she'll get over it."

———

Over the next week it becomes clear that Josie won't be *getting over it* anytime soon. She hasn't called, texted or come by and I'm not the only one who notices. We're having dinner at home with our moms when both Debbie and Paula comment on how odd it is for her not to at least call for so long.

I shift in my chair, hoping my guilt isn't written all over my face.

Gabe glances over at me before he says, "She called a few days ago. Her brother is in town."

Debbie looks relieved. "Oh that's nice. I'm sure she's happy to have him back for a little while. He lives in New York, right?"

I shovel in another mouthful of salad and try not to feel hurt. Her brother being in town has nothing to do with why she hasn't come by. We haven't gone this long without seeing Jo in years and she's had any number of family members in town since then. After talking with Gabe, I've been thinking a lot about the way we treat her.

She's trying to be taken seriously with her photography and I haven't done a great job of supporting that. I went to her show but I've given her plenty of grief over the nudity thing. Gabe has been more supportive but he's always had a tendency to treat her like a little girl who needs to be protected instead of a grown woman in charge of her own destiny.

In hindsight I can see a lot of ways that Gabe and I both haven't been respectful of her decisions in general. No wonder she's ignoring us.

"Isn't that right, Zack?"

My attention snaps back to the table. My mom points to my plate. "It's good, right? I got the tomatoes you like this time."

I look down at my plate and nod dumbly. But whatever I've agreed to must make some sense because she turns to Debbie and laughs at something she said. I need to snap out of it before anyone else notices my strange mood and makes the connection between my funky attitude and Josie's absence.

This is exactly what I was worried about happening. Josie and I being at odds puts the entire dynamic of my family at risk. I have to fix this. Going to see her is the only solution because she hasn't answered any of my calls or texts. It's time we put this to rest.

When I look up Sasha is watching me closely.

After dinner, I slip out before anyone can ask me what I'm doing. If I let things go on too long, Gabe will eventually go over there. The last thing I want is him finding out about our makeout session on her floor. He's weirdly protective of her and would immediately assume the worst. I just need to talk to her. Apologize for the things I've said. Accusing her of pulling a stunt to grab Gabe's attention seems pretty stupid in hindsight.

In light of the things I know now, everything I said to her that day was pretty shitty.

I park a few houses down and walk over. My car right in front of the house won't help if she's avoiding me. I knock and then keep my back turned so only my profile is visible.

The door swings open and Isabelle looks shocked. "Oh. Hi."

"Can I talk to Jo? Please tell her it won't take long."

She doesn't look convinced so I tack on, "Five minutes. I promise."

"Fine. Come on in." She steps back so I can enter the foyer and then walks up the stairs. I stand uncomfortably in the open listening to the soft murmur of voices above me. Probably Isabelle trying to convince Jo to come down. A few minutes later, Josie appears at the head of the stairs.

"What do you want, Zack?"

Again with the loaded questions.

"Five minutes of your time to apologize."

"Apology accepted. Consider your conscience clear."

"Josie, please."

She sighs and then walks down the stairs, clutching her robe around her neck. Up close she looks tired and her eyes are slightly red which really makes me feel like a dick.

"Okay, I'm here. You really don't have to say anything else. I know you're sorry."

"But you don't know what I'm sorry for. I'm sorry about ruining your thing with the models. This is your profession and I should have respected that."

She shrugs. "Maybe hiring someone isn't the right way to go. Last time I used volunteers and I was really happy with the results."

"Still, I shouldn't have just barged in. You're a grown woman and I know your art is important to you. I'm going to try harder to respect that. I'm also really sorry for what I said about you trying to break up Gabe and Sasha. That was a horrible thing to say."

Her eyes fill suddenly and that almost breaks me. Seeing her in tears and knowing that I'm the cause is one of the lowest points of my life.

"Thank you, Zack. That means a lot. Because that really hurt me."

I pull her into a hug. She resists it at first and then her arms wrap around my waist. With her shuddering sigh all the tension seems to melt from her body.

"I'm truly sorry, Jo."

After a few minutes she pulls back. Her smile is slightly embarrassed. "Any chance we can just forget all of this ever happened?"

"Not a chance."

Her eyes jump to mine. Then it's back, the same crackling tension in the air that was there right before she kissed me for the first time. Her robe falls open as I pull her into my arms. She's only wearing boxers and a thin T-shirt. No bra. I can feel her nipples against my chest.

"I'm not sorry for leaving when I did. I still think that we would have regretted it if I'd done what I really wanted to do."

"What did you want to do?" Her arms curl around my neck and she doesn't pull away when I open my legs so she can settle between them.

"I wanted to rip that shirt off you and see if your nipples look the way I've imagined they do. I wanted to let you keep riding me but without my jeans in the way. You have no idea how many dirty things I want."

Her eyes drift closed. "I want to know. So much."

Her lips part slightly and I pull her closer to kiss her softly. She lets out a little sigh when I stroke my tongue over her bottom lip. The kiss starts off soft but quickly flames out of control. My hand comes up to cup a heavy breast, the weight perfect in my palm. She gasps when I brush my thumb over her nipple.

"Is it okay that I'm kissing you?" I ask in between panting breaths.

Her fingers are working some kind of magic on the back of my neck so I'm thinking she's really okay with it. But I don't want to make any assumptions here. This is too important.

"More than okay. I told you, I'm not the one who's confused."

I pick up her hand and bring it to my lips. "I have no right to ask for a favor but I'm doing it anyway."

"What is it?"

"If you hire someone for this thing, I'll worry about you every day. I still want you to use me. I realize I may not be what you were looking for but..."

"All that ink makes for a pretty interesting canvas. You're perfect, Zack. You're everything I've been looking for."

Her words have a double meaning now and I'm reminded again why it's so important that I don't fuck this up.

"I've been thinking about what you said. About wanting to just live your life and be happy. To have some adventures. Let's do that."

She pulls back, an amused smile on her lips. "You want to help me have adventures?"

"Yeah. I need to get used to you taking my picture so maybe you can bring your camera while we do stuff."

"What kind of stuff?"

"Fun stuff. Whatever we feel like doing. Let's start with getting you out of the house. Go get dressed." I pop her on the bottom.

She raises an eyebrow but turns and goes back upstairs. Five minutes later she comes back down in tight jeans, a sweater and a faded blue ball cap with her ponytail pulled through the back. She grabs a hooded zip-up jacket from the stand by the door. Her camera bag is hanging there as well. I grab it and hand it to her.

"Adventure time starts now."

———

*J*osie follows me to my car. She doesn't ask any questions but I can tell she's carefully considering everything. I'm not even sure where I'm taking her I just know that we need to be alone. Before I even know what I'm doing, I'm driving back toward Gabe's house. I park in the drive and then as we climb out of the car, I hold out my hand to Josie.

"Let's take a walk."

She accepts my hand and we walk together through his backyard. We keep going past his property line to the river that runs behind his house. I step on a rock in the center and then jump to the other side. One of my feet lands in the water.

"Fuck that's cold!"

I shake my foot, happy that I wore thick boots. The top of my sock is wet but if I'd been wearing sneakers my entire foot would have been soaked. Josie chuckles and then hops over and lands next to me gracefully. She tips her chin up to the sun and the look on her face is so peaceful. Then she opens her eyes and follows me as I lead us deeper into the woods.

As we walk, the dead leaves on the ground crunch under our feet. Josie burrows deeper into her jacket. I pull her under my arm, sharing my body heat. She looks up at me gratefully.

"This is exactly what I needed."

"Me, too. I've been going crazy this past week. I knew that I was wrong as soon as I left but I was trying to respect your wishes. You asked me to leave you alone so I left you alone. But it was really hard."

"I would have never guessed. You've always seemed so ... I don't know. Just like you don't care what anyone thinks. Whether it's getting another tattoo or shaving your head, you do what you want, when you want. I envy that."

"Don't. My rebellion was just as much a product of frustration as your willingness to follow. Ever since I was little, I've been poked and prodded. Doing what I wanted with my body the rest of the time was the only time I was in control of anything. You know how we grew up?"

She nods. I figured that Gabe had told her the story at least once.

"Well, people weren't always welcoming. Our moms' situation is unique and it can bring out the worst in people. With all the doctor visits to control my diabetes, it wasn't easy. Gabe's reaction was to become more charming. He became a master manipulator. He was determined to make people like him no matter what. Me? I was so tired and sick a lot of the time. I didn't have the energy to care about what anyone thought of us and after a while I decided it was better that way."

She leans against me and her hair brushes against my face. Normally I would shy away from this kind of intimacy but at this moment, in this place and time, it seems totally right to rest my head against hers and soak up all the warmth she offers. Being so close to her gives me the courage to broach the subject we've both been avoiding.

"You really dropped a bomb on me last week."

She groans. "That was totally embarrassing. I can't believe I even said all that stuff to you. I wish I could take it back."

"I don't. What you said... does that mean what I think it does? You've really never..."

"Had sex? That's a negative."

"Wow."

"I know. A twenty-one-year-old virgin. I've been compared to finding a unicorn in the wild." She rolls her eyes.

Trying to keep the laughter out of my voice is difficult but I'm really trying to have a serious conversation. "You never wanted to with anyone before?"

She shrugs. "Perry was great about it. He respected that I wanted to wait. But when he proposed, he wanted to, you know, for my twenty-first birthday. I was thinking about just letting him do it but then I would look at that picture, the one I showed you and I just... couldn't."

"I'm glad you didn't."

Her satisfied smile lets me know how she feels about that.

"Anyway, I decided that if I have to lie back and think of England the whole time then what the hell is the point? I don't want it to be something I close my eyes and suffer through."

"It should never be something you suffer through, Josie. If it's right, then you'll want to do it."

She looks up at me through her lashes. "I wanted to with you. That day."

A shudder runs through me. "I wanted to with you, too. This whole thing is unexpected. For years you were just Josie and then one day when I looked at you, I suddenly saw all this other stuff, too. But your first time shouldn't be on the floor. It should be special."

There's laughter in her eyes when she glances up at me. "I think it would have been pretty special. Besides, you're already my first in every other way. My first love. My first kiss."

"What? No, I wasn't."

"New Year's Eve five years ago. I was talking about how I didn't have anyone to kiss at midnight. You leaned over and said 'It's not that big of a deal' and laid one on me. That was my first kiss."

She quirks her eyebrows and then raises her camera. While I stand in the cold trying to figure out how I've been so oblivious, she takes my picture.

"Have I ruined everything between us? By telling you how I feel?" she asks softly. When she lowers the camera, I can see the fear in her eyes.

"I'm so scared to say the wrong thing. This past week without you around has been really hard. On all of us."

She looks chagrined. "I didn't mean to stay away so long. I especially wouldn't want to make Debbie and Paula worry. But I promise not to get mad no matter what you say. This is a judgment free zone."

"Sex changes things between people. It attaches a lot of expectations. Do you understand what I mean?"

Her cheeks tinge pink but she nods slowly.

"And I don't do relationships. I'm just not built for that. I've never cared enough."

"You're not that way with me."

"I hope not. I would never want to be that way with you. That's why I stopped things the other day."

She considers me for a long moment. The wind whips the hair hanging from her baseball cap until a long strand sticks to her cheek. Her color is high and she looks so vibrant. It would kill me if anything I did took that sparkle from her eyes.

Finally she says, "You're worried about what happens afterward."

"Yes, I am. I'm so afraid that I'll do something that hurts you."

"I'll be hurt more if I end up doing this with some guy I don't care about."

The sharp stab of jealousy takes me by surprise. My hands curl into fists at the thought of Josie wrapped around some other guy. I care about Jo too much to let her do something she'll regret. I'm still worried that she'll assume sex equals love, so many women do, but honestly that's a risk even if her first time is with someone else.

At least if she's with me her first time will be with someone who truly loves her and has her best interests at heart. And I'll finally be able to shake this obsession with her.

Suddenly my prior reservations seem stupid in comparison with what I'm gaining. It's a risk getting involved with a close friend but in this case, the reward is worth it.

"Since we're in a judgment free zone, I have to admit that the thought of you doing this with anyone else makes me crazy."

"Does it really?"

I laugh at her eager expression. "You know it does. You're a little temptress."

She looks smugly satisfied at that description. "So does this mean you're saying yes? You'll do it?"

"Yes. I'll do it. If this is really what you want, then I'd be honored to be your first. It's not like it's a hardship to make love to a beautiful woman. As long as you know that you can change your mind at any time and I'll respect that."

"I know that, Zack. As if you'd do anything else." Her eyes are bright as she looks up at me with a sassy smile. "So, should I say thank you?"

"Not yet, brat. You might not be thanking me when you find out some of the dirty things I've imagined doing to you." I let out a sigh of relief that the hardest part of the conversation is over and things don't seem too awkward yet.

"I can't wait." She blushes and then links her arm through mine. "You really want to know why it never happened before?"

"I want to know everything about you."

"With Gabe, I always followed his lead. He was my crutch. He made me feel safe because he kept me away from everything that scared me. For a long time that was what I needed but now, I want more from life. You don't make me feel safe."

"I bet."

She turns to look at me, her bright eyes shining. "You make me feel alive."

I have no idea what to say to that or how to handle the sudden urge to pick her up and run off with her. But I can't do that. The rest of the family will be relieved to see her and we need some distance between us after such an intense conversation. But when she's looking at me like this, I forget about everything else. It's unsettling the way she can disrupt my world with one look.

She raises her camera and takes a picture of what must be the most befuddled expression in existence. Because that's definitely how I feel.

"Come on, we need to get back. Everyone will be really happy to see you." I glance over at her as we turn around and walk back the way we came. "Did I really just agree to take your virginity?"

Her satisfied expression does funny things to my insides. It makes me think about other things I can do to put that look on her face.

"Yup. And there's no getting out of it now."

Chapter Eight

Josie

The entire walk back to Gabe's house, I'm convinced the last hour has been a dream. Did Zack seriously just agree to make love to me? The thought scares and excites me. All the things he said and warned me about hang in the back of my mind but the only thing that stands out is that tonight, I'll finally know what it's like to be in his arms.

When we reach the house, Zack opens the back door with his key. Debbie looks up when we enter. Her excited screech brings Paula and Sasha rushing into the kitchen, Gabe not far behind.

"Our girl is back! We've missed you, honey."

I'm folded into a warm hug before Paula grabs me, too. "Where have you been? It's not the same around here without your smiling face."

"Sorry I stayed away so long. I've missed you guys, too."

Gabe and Sasha watch indulgently as the kitchen becomes a jumble of excited laughter and talking. I glance over at Zack who is leaning against the wall. My breath stops at the look in his eyes but I can't allow myself to get caught up. Not when his family is right here watching our every move.

The warm welcome drives home his earlier point about how risky this is.

He's right to be scared of things possibly changing. But no matter how hard you try, nothing stays the same anyway. The earth keeps turning and life goes on. It'll hurt for sure if I can't show him how good things could be between us but I have to try. I've wanted Zack for so long and I know that I can't go forever in this state of limbo.

Once things settle down a bit, Sasha speaks up. "I'm glad you're here, Josie. Maybe these guys won't be such grumps now."

Sasha glances over at Zack who mutters a curse under his breath.

The news that Zack was grumpy while I wasn't around is strangely satisfying. He claims that he doesn't do relationships or emotions but there's so much love inside him. I've always known it's there. It's in the way he's always been there for me and the tender way he is with his family. He wants everyone to think he doesn't care about anything but anyone looking can see that isn't true.

"Anyway, I wanted to make sure you knew about my grand opening party for my new club. It's in three weeks and I want you all to be there."

Sasha told me previously about her new jazz club but with everything that's been going on lately, I hadn't realized it was opening so soon.

"Wow! The time has gone by so quickly. Congratulations."

She looks giddy. "We've had crews working overtime to get things ready. If your brother is still in town you should bring him. And your roommate, too."

"Will Perry be coming with you?" Debbie asks.

Zack's eyes lift to mine and even from across the room his stare sends shivers down my spine.

Gabe flinches and then makes a cutting motion at his neck. "Mom, they broke up."

Debbie covers her mouth. "Oh no, I'm so sorry!"

"Yeah, we did. With everything that's been going on I didn't get to tell you guys."

There's another round of commotion as I'm enveloped in hugs again, with everyone telling me how sorry they are. All the while, Zack watches with that maddening little smile on his face.

"It's okay, really. It was for the best."

Paula puts her arm around my shoulders. "It's better you found out he was a dud now rather than later. Maybe Sasha can fix you up!"

Sasha winks. "I could do that. But I don't think Josie will have any trouble finding her own dates."

Heat rushes to my cheeks. Sasha is the only other person there aware of how I feel about Zack. Even though I know she won't spill the secret, it's still incredibly uncomfortable to have this conversation play out while Zack watches.

After Debbie and Paula leave, Sasha and Gabe go back upstairs. He's still moving slowly but I'm happy to see he's looking much better than the last time I saw him.

Once we're alone, I turn to Zack. "That was a little awkward."

"Just think, we'll have a lifetime of awkwardness to look forward to."

Or we could have a lifetime of something else. But I don't say that out loud. If I want him to give this a chance, scaring him with thoughts of commitment isn't the way to go.

"Are you backing out of our deal?"

Zack looks like he wants to but finally he shakes his head. "No. But I do have one condition. We can't tell Gabe."

"Am I your dirty little secret?" I'm joking but there's a little pang of hurt at the idea that he doesn't want to be seen with me.

"It's no one's business. It'll only make them uncomfortable and trust me, they'll all have an opinion about it."

I think about how weird it was to have Debbie and Paula asking about my dating life before. It would be doubly weird for them to know that I'm doing the nasty with Zack. Just the thought of that makes me want to go hide.

"That's probably for the best then."

"Come on, I'll drive you home."

He puts his hand on my lower back as we walk outside. My stomach is instantly a mass of butterflies. I can hardly believe what's about to happen. Are we really going to do this? My mouth is suddenly dry and I'm hit with a million insecurities at once. Will he be expecting sexy lingerie? Did I remember to shave this morning? What if it hurts a lot and I can't even do it?

All these thoughts swirl around my brain the entire drive home until I'm a ball of nerves when he finally parks in front of Izzie's house.

"What's wrong with you? You look like you're on the way to an execution."

Zack waits patiently as I figure out how to explain what I'm feeling without coming off as completely flighty. I've assured him over and over that this is really what I want and now that we're about to get down to it, I'm terrified.

"I'm just nervous. But it's no big deal. Everyone's nervous their first time, right?"

Zack cracks up. "Jo, what do you think is about to happen?"

He cracks up harder when I glare at him. I mean, seriously what does he think?

"I thought you'd want to, you know, do it now."

"Eager little thing, aren't you?"

"Well... yeah."

His smile flashes again before he reaches over and takes my hand. The butterflies in my stomach explode all over again at the warm press of his palm against mine.

"I'm eager, too sweetheart but I want it to be right. It should never be something you do on a schedule. When the time is right, it'll just happen. We're not going to rush it."

"So, you're not coming in?"

He shakes his head. Even though I'm disappointed there's an equal part of me that's relieved also. When we were kissing on the floor the other day, I was too into it to be nervous. Everything was all warmth and sensation and there was no room in there for nerves. But just doing it out of the blue is really intimidating. Trust Zack to know that I'd feel that way. He always seems to know what I'm feeling. Although he's usually using those insights to annoy me.

"I'm not going to make love to you, yet. But I am going to kiss you."

He leans over halfway and waits for me to make the next move. I lean into him and when our lips meet, it warms me down to my toes. He doesn't try to turn it into anything else either, no tongue or hands involved. Just a sweet kiss that makes me feel completely cherished.

Until in a moment of bravery, I pull his lip between my teeth.

He moans into my mouth and just that quickly, the kiss turns hot and wet. His tongue slides against mine and I suck on it gently.

Zack pulls back, his heavy breathing loud in the quiet car.

"Go in the house, Josie. Before I change my mind about being a gentleman."

"I don't want you to be a gentleman."

"Go," he growls.

I can feel his eyes on me until I enter the house and shut the door behind me. By the time I slide into bed later that night, I swear I can still feel his lips on mine.

Chapter Nine

Josie

Two days go by before we have time to meet again. Zack asks me to come to the shop. I have no idea what to expect. Guys usually have a different idea of taking things slow so I'm not sure what he's planning for later. Just in case, I take extra time conditioning my hair and shave my legs so they are perfectly smooth.

When I get to my bikini line I have another minor freak out. Izzie's always talking about getting waxed but I'm too scared to do that. Is that what guys expect now? For it to be completely bare down there?

"This is way too much stress," I mumble before deciding to just do my usual routine, cleaning up the stray hairs. I like things tidy but have never felt the need to take it all off before. I hope Zack is cool with the natural look.

As I dry my hair I think about our conversation last night. He called me right before bed and we stayed on the phone for an hour just chatting about random things. He didn't bring up our deal and neither did I but I'm sure it's not far from his thoughts.

Talking to him is different now. He's not being as raunchy as usual and he seems to be making an effort to ask about what's going on in my life. Usually he's teasing me or we're bickering about something but now, well, I think we're flirting.

I like it.

When I get to the shop, I pull around the back and park next to Zack's car. He drives this souped up electric blue Dodge Challenger that's as loud and in-your-face as he is. His leather jacket is visible on the passenger seat. I wonder if he's going to take me for a ride. He knows I love riding with him just because I love this car.

The back door requires a key so I walk around the front. My stomach is fluttering again. As many times as I've visited him or Gabe at the shop, this feels completely different. This time I'm here with no idea of what's going to happen.

This time I'm nervous.

The bell on the front door tinkles overhead when I enter. It seems way louder than usual. Zack is behind the counter and when he sees me, his face softens. He tips his head up acknowledging me before he turns back to his customer.

I have no idea how to act. I've always had a slightly antagonistic relationship with Zack. First because he made fun of me relentlessly for following Gabe around all the time. Then later because he made me hot which pissed me off.

Now we're at this strange detente and it's like starting over from scratch. After everything that happened when Gabe got injured, our previous state of feuding seems silly and juvenile.

But that doesn't mean I feel comfortable with him doing me favors. Especially not these kind of favors.

Thanks for getting naked for me so I can capture your incredible body on camera! And could you also rock my world between the sheets so I can see what all the fuss is about? Great, thanks!

It's all mortifying.

Since Zack is busy, I go in the back to say hi to everyone else. Jim waves as I pass by but doesn't stop what he's working on. When I cross the garage one of the mechanics, Reed Harris, waves me over. Zack told me once Reed was in their class in high school but I don't remember him from back then. He's got a laid back beach bum kind of vibe with messy blond hair that always looks like it needs a trim.

"Hey, girl. Where have you been lately? Haven't seen you for a while." He pulls me into a quick hug.

I shrug but I can feel the heat climbing to my cheeks. If you'd told me last week that my absence would be such a big deal, I wouldn't have believed it. It's nice to be missed though.

"Just busy. Had family in town and working on something new. What about you?" I deflect back to him, hoping he doesn't notice how shaky my voice is.

"It's been the same old thing around here. We're all working overtime while Gabe's out."

"Yeah. I know he misses you guys. He hates not being able to work."

"That was pretty messed up what happened to him."

No one outside of the family knows the real story behind Gabe's attack. Everyone else thinks he was mugged at random.

"It was. I'll be sure to tell him you asked about him. Once he's feeling better I'm sure he'd appreciate a visit."

He grins. "Sasha's with him so I won't go just yet. I'm sure he's enjoying being taken care of."

"Hey, Jo. Sorry about that."

We both turn at the sound of Zack's voice. He's still wearing the coveralls with his name stitched in the right corner and his dark hair has started to grow in on the sides a bit. Without the spikes and the tattoos on display, he almost looks... normal.

"Hey. It's okay."

Reed looks back and forth between us. "Cool, I have to get back to work. But I'll see you around."

Zack leads me to the other side of the garage where a black motorcycle is waiting in one of the bays.

"Nice bike. What kind is it?"

"This is a Harley Softail."

"Who does it belong to?"

"One of our longtime customers, Helen Chisholm. She's a great lady and she's been coming here for a long time. Reed just finished this one. I wanted to take it for a spin and make sure it's good to go. I figured that would be an adventure."

I gape at him. "You want me to ride that?"

"Not by yourself. With me. Have you ever ridden before?"

"No. Gabe never takes his bike when we go out. I only asked him once and he said that he didn't want to risk it. That he's not used to having anyone ride with him."

"He was lying. I've ridden behind him before and we were fine. You have to understand that Gabe has more old-fashioned ideas than I do. He thinks that women should be protected. He hasn't taken Sasha on his bike either."

"You don't think women need to be protected?"

He shrugs. "Sometimes I do. But there's a difference between being protected and being put on a shelf. What's the point of living life from the backseat?"

Zack reaches behind me and picks up a helmet. It's black with these cool blue designs running down the sides. "You'll need this."

I hand him my bag which he stashes in a drawer. I finally lose my grip on my excitement and let out a little squeal.

"This is so cool! Are you sure the owner won't mind?"

Zack helps me position the helmet over my hair. I had it up in a ponytail which I have to take down to get the helmet to fit.

"I'm sure she won't mind because I called and asked her. Usually I would take it up the street and back but I wanted to really take you for a ride."

I give him a saucy look. "Are we still talking about motorcycles?"

"I am but I've learned not to underestimate your imagination, Miss Harlow."

The low timbre of his voice combined with the soft touches of his fingers against my chin as we finally get the helmet in place set my stomach tingling again. But I'm very aware that we're not alone.

Jim has come out from under the car he was working on. He's brought his customer to the back to show him something under the hood. He only glances our way briefly but the man sees everything, always has. And Reed is pretending to be looking for something in his toolbox but every time I look over there, he's watching us.

Now I feel completely self-conscious, sure that everyone around me can read my feelings for him as surely as if they're written all over my face.

"Everyone is staring."

Zack snorts. "No, they're not."

"This is weird. I feel like I'm suddenly seeing spies on every corner when any other day I would have come back here to talk to you without even thinking about it."

Zack hits a button and the automatic door for our bay opens. He climbs on the bike and then gestures for me to get on behind him. He shows me where to put my feet.

"They're only staring because we're not fighting for once."

"We don't fight that much, do we?"

"All the time. You gave me hell."

"You deserved it."

We laugh together. This flirting thing is way more fun than arguing ever was.

"Besides," Zack continues. "He's just jealous that he doesn't have Jessica Rabbit snuggled up to him."

"Jessica Rabbit was a redhead," I point out.

"Was she?"

"Yes."

"I'll take your word for it. Believe me, I wasn't looking at her hair."

"Oh, I know what you were looking at."

I laugh and then squeal when he starts the engine. I grab him around the waist. I would have never thought this would be a sensual experience but between the hard press of Zack's back and the rumble between my thighs, I have an entirely new understanding of why people like motorcycles.

"Are you ready?"

I tap his stomach twice to let him know I'm okay. He pulls out and the wind swallows my scream.

———

Over the next week, we embark on a series of adventures with me taking pictures along the way. Some are thrilling, some are silly but every single one is more fun than I've had in ages.

After our afternoon of motorcycle riding, the next day we went to a carnival and rode the Ferris wheel and lost money playing all those *obviously* rigged games. Then he took me to a gym in the neighboring city of New Haven that has a rock wall. We spent the afternoon racing to see who could climb to the top the fastest. He won every time.

I know what he's doing. He's making sure I'm comfortable and that I won't regret anything. He's being so sweet and patient. With every one of our adventure dates, I'm more sure than ever that my heart knew what it was doing when it decided on Zack Marshall.

Even though I appreciate his patience, the burn has increased with every hour that I'm with him. Now every touch puts me on edge. Every time he brushes against me, I'm on fire. I want him.

And I'm ready.

When he tells me that he wants to stay home on Friday night, I know that the time has come. There's no man in the world who can hold out this long and frankly if he doesn't do something tonight then I might take matters into my own hands. I'm rushing around cleaning the house, straightening things and I've changed my shirt several times.

My brother is sitting at the table in the kitchen. He watches my mania with curious eyes. "Why do you keep wiping that counter? You've been at that same spot for the past ten minutes."

"This place is filthy! I'm just cleaning up."

Jamie looks around. "It looks fine. You weren't this OCD when I lived at home."

Izzie looks over at me with knowing eyes. I told her that Zack was coming over earlier because she wanted to know if I had plans. Her usual drinking partners have done the unthinkable and all gotten boyfriends. This has put a serious dent in her partying.

Luckily she takes pity on me. I think she can tell that I'm really nervous and on the verge of having some kind of breakdown.

"Women get on these random cleaning binges sometimes. I do it, too when I have PMS."

He shakes his head. "Women are a mystery."

"I have an idea. James, why don't we go to the movies? I'll even buy the popcorn."

Relief sweeps through me and I give Izzie a grateful look. The thought of doing sexy things while they're around freaks me out. What if they heard us? My brother and I are cool but there are some things that I will never feel comfortable talking about with him. I'll be way less stressed if Zack and I have the house to ourselves.

"It's been a long time since I've done that," Jamie says. "That would be great. Yes, let's do it." He looks really excited.

I could just hug Izzie for this. She can be pushy and brash sometimes but she's always there for me. Entertaining my brother is way above and beyond the call of friendship. Jamie is pretty conservative and I've noticed that Izzie has tried to tone down her more outrageous traits while he's around.

Fifteen minutes later they are gone and I'm waiting in the living room having finally given up on achieving a perfectly clean kitchen. When Zack knocks on the door a few minutes later, I yank it open right away.

He looks at me and then behind him. "Am I late?"

"No. I was just right here. That's all."

He follows me inside and I wait while he hangs his coat on the stand. Then he turns and pulls me into his arms. Our kiss quickly turns hot and I'm practically climbing him where he stands. He pulls back slightly and licks his lips.

"Missed me, huh?"

"Yeah. I have." Suddenly hit with nerves after almost climbing down his throat, I lead him into the living room. "Do you want anything to drink?"

He claps his hands. "No, I think I'm good."

I notice that he's freshly shaved and he's taken the time to change out of the T-shirt and jeans he usually wears under his coveralls at work. The jeans he's got on now look brand new and his shirt is a button up. His hair has been buzz cut so it's all the same length for once. It dawns on me then that he's cleaned up for me.

He's nervous, too.

"So, how was work today?" I sit on the couch and pat the cushion next to me.

"Good. I think we're finally caught up for once. Gabe has been doing some of the admin stuff from home now that he's feeling better."

"That's great. I had a pretty good day, too. I've been editing some of the photos I took of you that first day."

That gets his attention. "Really? Can I see them?"

I smile to myself. This is perfect because he'll have to come to my room. I couldn't have planned that better.

"Sure. Come on. Some of them are pretty good."

He follows me up the stairs and into my room. I close the door behind him and he sits on the bed while I open my laptop. The photo I was working on last is still open on the screen. I bring it over to the bed and angle the screen so he can see them.

"It's strange to see myself this way. I've never really liked taking pictures."

"You're extremely photogenic. I'd love to get some shots of you the next time you shave your head. The tattoos on your head paired with the Mohawk are one of my favorite looks on you."

He runs a hand over his short hair. "And here I've been growing it out thinking you'd like that better."

It's the first tacit admission that he's been trying to please me. It's a heady feeling to know that my preference matters that much to him. Especially since he rarely cares what anyone thinks.

I continue scrolling through the pictures, showing him all the ones from that first day and then the ones I took on our walk through the woods the day he apologized. My favorite is the one when I told him he was my first kiss. When we get to the end, there's a new appreciation in his eyes when he looks at me.

"I am so proud of you, Josie. These are fantastic."

"Thank you." Plenty of people have told me I'm a talented photographer but it means something altogether different to hear it from Zack. Because I care what he thinks.

"Can I see more of your work?" he asks shyly.

"Sure, of course. I have tons of photo albums."

I walk into the closet and stand on tiptoe to reach the albums on the top shelf. For years, I collected photos of everything around me. Nature, people, cars. Anything and everything. I was waiting for something to inspire me. It wasn't until I started photographing families that I felt the connection I've always been missing.

The first book I pull down has shots of several of my parents' friends with their kids. I flip through the first few pages, smiling at the images of children at play and parents sneaking a kiss while they thought no one was looking. Looking at these now, I can see all the technical mistakes I made back then. But the emotion in these pictures practically jumps from the pages.

I wander back into the room holding the book open to one of my favorite shots. "These are some of my earliest attempts. You might remember my friend Hailey from–"

Zack looks up from the photo album open on his lap. The album that's usually under my bed. The one that I've never shown anyone.

"Josie..." He stares at me and then glances back down at the album.

Even upside down I can tell which picture he's looking at. It was taken one day when we were teenagers and Gabe had the grand idea to try to pop wheelies on this old motorcycle Zack had fixed up. In the photo, Zack is watching his brother with a look of patient affection. He looks happy.

"I look so young in this picture. When was this taken?"

"Um, that was the summer when my parents made me take ballroom lessons so that must have been when I was about sixteen. So you would have been about nineteen."

The wonder in his eyes when he looks up at me takes me by surprise. "I didn't even know you had a camera. Obviously you had a camera a lot of times when I wasn't paying attention."

He's referring to the fact the entire album is filled with pictures of him. Nothing but pictures of him. Most of them taken at times when he wasn't even aware I was photographing him.

It's a little embarrassing that he's found this. But it's the only definitive proof of what I told him. That my feelings for him aren't a new thing.

"Teenage girls can be a little obsessive. It's a good thing you didn't find this back then. You would have gotten a restraining order."

"I wouldn't have minded, even then." He tugs on a lock of my hair. "I think that's why I was so mean to you sometimes. Gabe took you for granted and it killed me because I always knew I couldn't compete with him for your heart."

"You didn't have to win my heart. You've always had it," I whisper.

He leans in and this time when he kisses me, he doesn't stop.

Chapter Ten

Zack

$\mathcal{I}$ would have thought that nothing could surprise me at this point in my life. I've gotten used to living life behind a wall. Caring about nothing and no one because it was easier than being disappointed over and over again.

But seeing that album of pictures took me completely off guard. There was a very real fear in the back of my mind that Jo was only with me because her first choice wasn't available. That I was some sort of consolation prize. But a simple book of pictures has convinced me of her sincerity in a way that nothing else could.

She has an entire album of me. There's no denying that this was a work of love done with all the intensity of a teenage crush.

Those pictures prove that she was telling the truth. I'm first in her heart and always have been.

As I'm kissing her, I feel my walls crumbling and all the emotion I've spent years hiding from seeps out. Her hair flows around us in a mass of brunette waves and I gather it in my fists, using it like an anchor to hold her close. Now that she's here I don't want her to ever leave me. She's just as intense, kissing and sucking like she can't get enough of my taste.

I pull back only long enough to help her out of her jeans and long tunic top. When she drops her arms, she grabs me again fusing our lips in another deep kiss. Somehow I manage to get my shirt off too. We're both taking gasping breaths between kisses, not wanting to stop long enough for anything more. I know a brief moment of frustration trying to toe my boots off when one gets stuck. Finally it pops free and lands on the floor with another loud thud.

Somehow I manage to turn us around so she's reclining on the bed. As she settles back I come down over her, holding up my weight on one arm while the other explores. There's so much to touch and taste. I place a trail of soft kisses down her neck until I get to the front clasp of her bra.

When I look up, Jo is watching me with wide, watchful eyes.

"Do it, Zack. I want you to," she whispers.

I unclip her bra and her breasts spring free. As my lips trail down her torso, her back arches pushing her plump breasts out for me like an offering. She's built like a dream with full, berry tipped nipples and creamy skin. As many times as I've imagined this, I couldn't have imagined how sexy she actually is. I spend long moments tormenting the sharp points of one nipple before switching to give attention to the other side.

Josie squirms beneath me. She's rocking her hips, rubbing her pussy against me like she's trying to get me inside. She's so with me right now and for the first time I find myself fighting for control pretty early in the process. Usually I have way more endurance than this but it's been a long time since I've teased myself with a straight week of foreplay first.

When I bite down on the plump nipple between my lips, Jo lets out a soft, agonized cry that goes straight to my dick. I pause, to give her a chance to settle and also to make sure I don't come in my pants.

"You okay?"

I raise my head to check on her. Her lips are slightly parted and her eyes are squeezed shut.

When she opens them and sees me looking, she manages a shaky smile.

"*So okay*. So incredibly okay."

Her enthusiastic response spins my need even higher. I've never been this nervous getting naked with a woman. But this is Josie. My Josie. Not only am I afraid of hurting her but I want her to love everything we do together. I want her to love it and want to do it again and again. The stakes have never been higher.

I tug her panties down slowly and she lifts her hips to help me get them off. Her fingers tug my hair insistently, urging me back to her breast. I give her what she wants, more deep suctioning pulls on her nipple that have her writhing beneath me again.

She's so sensitive that she might even be able to come just from this but there's so much more to touch and taste. The fragrant expanse of her skin calls to me and I continue sucking and licking all the way down the smooth expanse of her stomach. As I get lower, her soft little moans get longer and longer. When I finally scoot all the way down her legs fall open eagerly. I arrange her legs over my shoulders and get comfortable. She trembles beneath me.

I lick her from top to bottom in one long stroke. The taste of her takes me by surprise. I swallow a groan and then go back for more. When I take her clit on my tongue she goes completely still and then shudders, a full body tremor that seems to come from her core.

"Zack. *Oh my god.*" She whispers it in a reverent tone, like she can't believe the pleasure.

I can feel my ego inflating. *Yes.* This is what I want, to show her what her body is capable of and then get her addicted to the way I make her feel. So she'll only feel this with me.

She cries out again and again, her fingers curling desperately into the short strands of my hair, trying to find something to hold on to. Her nails scratch my scalp and I moan at the sensation. I introduce one finger, pushing into her tight, wet heat slowly, giving her time to get used to the sensation. She whimpers at the invasion but I lick her clit to distract her from where my finger is carefully stretching her.

"Does it hurt, sweetheart? Tell me if it does."

Her head shakes back and forth wildly. *"Don't stop!"*

I chuckle at her insistence. "I won't stop. Not now. Not when I know how good you feel."

She clenches around my finger at the words and I have to pause and take a breath when my dick pulses dangerously beneath me. I need to summon some measure of control if I have any chance of making this good for her. With her thighs around my head and her nails on my scalp, I'm aware that I hold her pleasure in my hands.

But god, the way she feels. It's so hard to think when she's whimpering beneath me. I love this, all of it, especially the sensation of being surrounded by her.

"You feel amazing sweetheart, so tight and wet. I can't wait to feel this sweet little pussy clenching when I'm deep inside you."

My dirty words only make her clench around me harder. When I flick her clit on my tongue over and over she comes immediately, shivering against me. I hold her in place, forcing her to take each lash of my tongue until she collapses, boneless and replete.

I raise my head and the look of complete exhaustion on her face is exactly what I want to see. My woman utterly satisfied.

The condoms I brought are in my pocket. I grab them and put the second one on her nightstand. Her eyes open and she surveys me lazily as I push my jeans and boxers down. A very satisfied smile covers her lips.

"You really are perfect. Look at you."

I realize that it's the first time she's seen my tattoo in its entirety. The legs of the phoenix extend past my waist and the feet and talons wrap around my groin. She extends a hand and touches the part that covers my ribs.

"It's extraordinary. It's almost a shame you have to cover it."

"I don't think I'd get much done if I didn't."

Her chest shakes with her laughter. "Definitely not. All the women coming to the shop would be there for more than just getting their cars serviced."

"Brat. That wasn't what I meant."

"I know. But that's what would happen. You are one sexy package, Zack Marshall."

Her fingers trail lower. My head falls back on my shoulders as she takes me in her hand, then touches the tip, rubbing through the moisture that's gathered there. At my harsh groan, she snatches her hand back.

"You're so hard," she whispers.

"Getting harder every second."

I kick my jeans away from my feet and roll on the condom. When I climb back in the bed, she looks up at me trustingly. I rest my forehead on hers and flex my hips until I'm resting right at her entrance. The heat of her arousal almost unmans me. Every inch of me wants to just dive right into what I know is about to be the tightest pussy I've ever breached. But I grit my teeth and hold myself still.

"If anything hurts—"

"It won't," she assures me.

"Or if you want to stop for any reason—"

Her hips arch up so I'm forced into her a few inches. All my will to go slow disintegrates as my cock is enveloped in her wet heat. She lets out a cry and her legs tighten behind my ass. Her muscles tighten instinctively around me as if trying to keep me inside. I have no defense against the iron tight grip she's got on my cock.

"Oh fuck."

She melts beneath me as I sink deeper. I bury my face in her shoulder and rock slowly, circling my hips to open her up. Her hands travel over my shoulders and into my hair. I sneak a look at her face, looking for signs of pain or discomfort. Her mouth is open and every time I push home, she lets out a soft sigh.

Before long I'm pushing in rhythmically until in one stroke she finally takes my full length. It feels so good that I feel like the virgin, completely innocent to how good it could be. Her pussy holds me lovingly, rippling and sucking me deeper and deeper with every stroke. Josie lets out another one of those soft cries that I'm helpless against and one of her hands slides down to my ass. She's holding me to her tightly. Like she wants it all.

The thought is so arousing that before I know what I'm doing, I push into her faster. My control is shot and I'm pure instinct, trying to make sure that every inch of our skin is in contact. Her legs curl around my waist and I hit a spot deep inside that pulls a long cry from her. I reach between us and rub her clit rhythmically. Moments later, she stiffens beneath me and then dissolves into a shivering orgasm that tightens all of her muscles simultaneously.

I don't stand a chance against watching her come apart beneath me. With the sound of her cries still in my ears, I give in and come too.

We fall off the edge together and the pleasure feels like it never ends.

I wish I could say that we spent long hours stroking each other and basking in bliss. Unfortunately we're interrupted by the unmistakable sound of the door slamming downstairs. Josie raises her head listening. Then every muscle in her body jerks. Not in a sexy way, either.

"Oh my god, they're back early!"

"What?"

She slaps a hand over my mouth. "*Shh*, they'll hear you."

The way she's moving around is doing interesting things to me since I'm still inside her. I'm half hard again just feeling her clench and tighten around me. Her expression turns from shock to disbelief as she looks down at where we're still joined.

"*Seriously?*"

I wink at her then grasp the edge of the condom before I withdraw. "I aim to please."

She watches with interest as I wrap the condom in a tissue and place it in the small trashcan beneath her desk. When I stand up again, her eyes are still on me.

"You definitely did that," she murmurs in that throaty way that makes me want to get back inside her again.

I listen and hear the sound of footsteps moving around below us. Then the sound of the television. It's clear that wherever her brother and roommate were before, they're back in for the night. Which means that the round two I was planning for Josie will have to wait. Josie sits up pulling the sheet over her breasts. The move makes me smile.

I lean down and nuzzle her ear. "Already seen it all. There's no use hiding those beauties now."

She rolls her eyes. "I'm not hiding. Just not used to flashing them around."

I watch as she slides out of bed and then starts picking up the items on the floor. She pulls her bra back on and then her tunic. She's turning around in circles and I finally realize she's looking for her panties. The ones I threw over my shoulder. I retrieve them from the floor on the other side of the bed and hand them to her.

"Thanks," she whispers without looking at me. She steps into them and then pulls her jeans back on. I dress silently, watching as she mentally retreats right in front of me. Every item of clothing she puts on is like another layer of armor she uses to keep herself protected.

To hell with that.

"Are you okay? Truly okay?" I stop her fidgeting by pulling her closer until her hands are trapped between us. Her hair is wild in the back where it was rubbing against her pillow and I tame the strands with my hands. "I want you to always be honest with me if you aren't happy. Or aren't satisfied."

She blushes deeply and buries her face in my shirt. "Not satisfied? Were you just here a few minutes ago?"

"I just wanted to make sure. You're not looking at me all of a sudden."

"Zack, I'm completely mortified that if they'd come home any earlier they would have heard me screaming the walls down. I wouldn't have even heard them come in. You make me forget myself completely."

My arms tighten around her. It makes me feel proud, and also deeply satisfied to know that I gave her what she needed.

"That's the way it should be. So no thinking of England then, huh?"

She laughs softly. "Definitely not. The only thing I was thinking was how to keep you right where you were."

"Believe me, sweetheart nothing could have dragged me away. Unfortunately this means that we can't do it again but maybe that's for the best. I'm greedy for you but you'll be sore tomorrow as it is."

She curls against me. "I don't care."

"I do. I never want to hurt you. Only give you pleasure." I sit on the edge of the bed. "Do you mind if I look at that album again?"

She looks shocked but picks it up from the floor where it fell. I accept the book and start from the beginning instead of the middle like last time. Looking at these photos is like taking a visual stroll down memory lane. Some of the pictures are events that I wasn't even aware she knew about.

My first coffee shop performance. That was before I figured out that I hate playing in front of strangers. Some people have a deep-seated need to share their love of music and that's great. There are so many musicians that I love listening to and I'm really glad they want to share. But for me, it's not necessary. I play because it soothes me. Managing stress is important to my health and playing the guitar calms me.

Josie captured the fear in my expression perfectly. If anyone else had taken this photo it would feel like a violation. But she's managed to capture the moment in such a way that you feel like a sympathetic friend instead of a voyeur. Like you're sharing in my fear and disappointment.

As I flip each page, my heart opens just a little more. I can feel the love in the pages as she's chronicling a life she desperately wants to share. Every image in this book is a reminder. No one has ever made me feel this way. No longer second best. I think back to what she told me before.

"You don't have to win my heart. You've always had it."

Josie has been arranging the sheets and blankets behind me. I stand so she can smooth the bedspread. The room looks the way it did when I arrived. After listening at the door, she opens it and then opens her laptop. If anyone comes upstairs, it will look like we're just hanging out.

After about ten minutes, footsteps sound on the stairs and Josie glances over at me. Her brother James passes by and then backtracks when he sees me sitting on the bed.

"Hey, Zack. I haven't seen you in a long time."

I stand and accept his handshake. "It has been a long time. It's great to see you again."

James looks over at the images of me on Josie's laptop. "So you're Jo's next subject?"

He raises his eyebrows. I hold his gaze as I nod. Josie's parents haven't been supportive but she's never mentioned if her brother has an issue with her new direction. If he does, then I'll be here to rip him a new one.

After an uncomfortable moment, he finally glances over at Jo. "So how did your session go?"

Josie sighs. "Do you really want to know?"

He appears to think about it. "Never mind. I'll just say, 'hope it was successful' and leave it at that."

He salutes and then backtracks to the hall. A few seconds later, I hear a door close.

I turn to her. "On that note, I should probably go."

"I wish you didn't have to."

"Believe me, I wish I didn't have to, either. But I don't think your brother is going to believe that we're working overnight."

She giggles and gets up from the desk. "Next time I'll actually take some photos of you."

"It'll be easier to take my clothes off then. And then I'll take *your* clothes off afterward."

She moves sensually as she crosses the room and when she stands on tiptoe to kiss me, she makes sure her breasts brush against my chest in a slow drag. My breath comes out in a soft huff when she grabs my ass and squeezes.

There's a glint in her eyes that I've never seen before as she says, "Promise?"

I think I've created a monster.

Chapter Eleven

Josie

$\mathcal{I}$ walk him downstairs. The television is on blaring a commercial at top volume but there's no one on the couch or in the kitchen. Jamie must have left it on. Izzie is nowhere in sight.

Zack pulls his coat off the stand and shucks into it. I watch his movements, especially his mouth. Desire rises again when I realize he probably still smells like me.

"Drive safely."

It's a thing I've said to him a thousand times but suddenly seems really intimate. I'm guessing that everything is going to seem really intimate from now on. I know what he looks like naked. I know how he feels inside me. There's no way to go back to what life was like before.

No way at all.

He crosses the room to me. Prowling is the only word for it. He's all swagger and rolling hips and *oh my* is it hot as hell.

"Can I come by tomorrow?"

An enthusiastic yes is on my lips until I realize the date.

"My parents' annual anniversary party is tomorrow night." I grasp the front of his coat and bury my face in his neck. "I really, really, *really* wish I could skip it now. It's always boring but now I'll be thinking about what I'm missing all night!"

There's no way I can pretend I forgot either since I know my mother will call tomorrow to remind me.

His chest rumbles beneath my cheek with his laughter. "Do you want me to come with you?"

My head shoots up. "Would you?"

"Sure, why not?"

"It's black tie. And at the country club," I add when he makes a *so what* face. "You'd be bored stiff within five minutes. I would never ask you to subject yourself to that on my behalf."

"I'm well aware that it'll be boring as hell. I'm offering to come anyway." He smiles down at me, his arms circling around my back to settle around my hips.

Even though I came, loudly, several times less than an hour ago, just being this close to him already has my motor purring again. What the hell has he done to me? One evening in my bed and Zack Marshall has turned me into a sex fiend.

"Well, you've been warned. It'll be nice not to look pathetic all night while everyone asks why I don't have a date. I'm assuming your tuxedo is already pressed and ready?"

He gives me a look.

"Just kidding." My giggles are cut off when he scoops me up in his arms playfully.

He sets me on my feet. "I'll buy one, brat."

"Will you be able to get one that fits that quickly?"

"You can get anything quickly if you have enough money." His face sobers but he quickly covers the look with a smile. It doesn't quite reach the corners of his eyes though and I recognize it for the mask it is.

Interesting.

After he found out about the money, Gabe ranted for days about their irresponsible father and how he's trying to buy their forgiveness. Underneath his anger, I could tell that he was actually a little hurt. That the father they've never known could just waltz in after years of absence like it was nothing was more hurtful to Gabe than he'd wanted to admit.

I could tell because I know Gabe so well, but Zack... he never seemed to care much about it either way. He's such a vault sometimes. All of his emotions are so carefully locked down but then there are these moments where you get a peek at what's beneath.

"Okay. So I'll pick you up tomorrow at..." He looks at me expectantly.

"The party starts at seven so pick me up around six. That should give us plenty of time."

"Okay. Then we'll pick up where we left off afterward. There's a lot of fun stuff we didn't get to tonight."

"Like what?" Of course I have a pretty good idea but I want to hear him say it. I love the way he talks dirty to me.

"Things I can't talk about if I have any hope of leaving you alone right now. I'm already halfway to booking a hotel and keeping you captive overnight. But I can't do that."

"Why not? You don't even have to take me captive. I surrender." I pull him down for another long kiss. My fingers curl against the back of his neck as our tongues tangle and slide against each other. Who could have ever guessed that smart mouth of his would be so talented at turning me on?

He breaks the kiss with a groan. "I'll remember you said that tomorrow night. Because I don't plan on going easy on you then."

"You'd better not. You're leaving me all hot and bothered here."

He pulls me closer and I can feel his erection beneath his jeans.

"I am, too. But tonight, when you're lying in your bed aching, you'd better not touch this." His hand presses between my thighs and his fingers curl into me, pressing my jeans into me slightly. A sudden throb of desire hits me so hard I sway against him.

"What? You can't tell me not to do that," I whisper, completely scandalized.

"I can and I am. *This is mine*. And I'll know if you're playing without me."

"How could you possibly know that?"

The private smile he gives me is so sexy my knees actually get weak. "Because I plan on talking to her again first thing next time. She'll tell me everything I need to know."

His thumb presses right against my clit and I can't stop the hoarse, achy sound that comes out of my throat. His eyes close, like he's savoring the sound.

"Goodnight, Josie."

He kisses me on the forehead and then he's gone.

———

By the next day I'm starting to wonder if I've made a mistake. Our country club is a microcosm of everything that I think is wrong with the world. A lot of self-important people trying to impress each other. I hate being there so why would I want to put Zack through the experience?

Gabe has accompanied me to several functions there before and I never thought anything about it. Gabe is ... well, he's Gabe. The man is a chameleon and he can fit in anywhere. But Zack doesn't care about fitting in.

This might just turn into a disaster.

I spend the afternoon at a photoshoot for a new client. I've been doing family portraits since I was seventeen and I've even done some wedding photography for friends of the family. I've always loved photographing people in love, capturing the beauty of deciding to spend your life with someone else. It's the most gutsy thing in the world to put your all into trusting someone else with your heart.

Today's client wants unique engagement photos so I take them to the train tracks on the edge of town. The two of them walking on the tracks makes for striking photos and the imagery is perfect. Starting a journey together. Traveling through life side-by-side. It's perfect. The couple is so much fun to shoot that I lose track of time and the afternoon flies by.

By the time I get home it's almost five o'clock. Izzie is downstairs watching television and James is in the kitchen eating a sandwich. When I enter the room, neither of them looks at me. There's a weird tension in the room, like I've just walked into the middle of an argument.

Izzie has been surprisingly cool about Jamie crashing here but I make a mental note to find out how long he plans to be in town. Having a house guest is always a bit of an adjustment and I don't want to impose on her hospitality for too long.

I set my camera bag down on one of the kitchen chairs and pull down a glass from the cabinet.

"What's going on?"

Jamie glances over and takes another huge bite of his sandwich. "Nothing," he mumbles.

I fill the glass at the sink and gulp down the water. "Okay, well I have to get ready to go."

I can't afford to show up late, either. My mother will definitely notice and she's already going to be shocked when she sees my date. I've never cared that Zack doesn't fit into the image of what my parents think is an appropriate partner for me but bringing him tonight is making a statement they won't be able to ignore. I'm not fooling myself that they'll be nice about it either.

Maybe I should just risk my mother's wrath by skipping tonight. Hearing her fuss tomorrow might be worth avoiding the drama that's sure to come tonight. Although Zack might be annoyed if I change my mind at the last minute. I mean, he had to go buy a tux just to come. My shoulders sag. The whole thing is so pretentious.

"Where are you going?" Izzie finally gets up and wanders into the kitchen. She sits at the kitchen table.

"We have our parents' anniversary party tonight. Zack is coming to pick me up in an hour. My photo shoot took longer than expected so I have to hurry. It'll take me at least an hour to shower and do my hair. Forget actually getting dressed."

"Zack is taking you? No wonder you're acting like such a nervous wreck."

"I'm not a wreck!" I almost drop the glass but manage to catch it. The little bit of water in the bottom sloshes out onto the floor.

Izzie gets up and takes the water glass from my hand. Jamie hands her a paper towel and she wipes up the mess on the floor.

"Sit down. You're making me nervous shaking like that."

I sit at the table and rest my head in my hands. "This is a bad idea."

She sits next to me and puts her hand on my shoulder. "Why? Tell me what's so bad about taking a guy you're crazy about with you to a family event?"

"You know how my parents are. They're so obsessed with appearances. Zack has never cared what anyone thinks and I love that about him. I just hate the idea of anyone making fun of him. Not because I care what they think but because I don't want him to have to put up with that crap because of me."

"Maybe you're worrying for nothing. I'm pretty sure Zack can handle himself."

"I know. You're totally right. He'll probably show up tonight with his hair in spikes wearing a purple tuxedo just to shake things up."

She laughs. "I'd love to see that. Your parents could use a little shaking up if you ask me."

Jamie pushes away from the counter. "Why don't you come with us? When I replied to the invitation a few months ago that was before Erica and I broke up. So I have two seats."

Izzie stares at him and then her eyes shift over to me. "Really? You don't mind?"

He pauses for an uncomfortably long time. Then says, "Of course not. It'll be fun. I bet our table will be the liveliest one there. I'm usually just pretending to pay attention. This will be the first time I'm actually having fun."

"Get dressed up and go to a fancy party? Twist my arm, why don't ya!"

We both laugh as Izzie runs upstairs, no doubt to tear apart her closet and find something to wear. A few minutes later Izzie yells down the stairs. "Jo, you'd better hurry up!"

I glance at the clock over the oven. "Oh, crap. She's right."

Zack will be here soon and I'll still be wearing jeans with my hair in a bun. I pat Jamie on the arm as I pass by.

"Thanks for inviting Izzie to come along. I know you did it to make me feel better and I appreciate it. It'll be nice to have a few people in my corner."

Jamie glances away, obviously uncomfortable with the praise. "It's no big deal. I want you to be happy. You have the right to be with who you want. If Zack is that guy, then I'll do whatever I can to help you out."

I leave him in the kitchen staring into space, probably wondering how he got roped into entertaining Izzie's crazy ass for the night.

Chapter Twelve

Josie

Zack still hasn't arrived by the time Izzie and Jamie leave. The extra time allows me to pin my hair up in a more complicated knot than usual and curl the tendrils of hair around my face. He likes my hair loose so I've left the front a little more messy than usual so the updo doesn't look so stiff.

I'm wearing a shimmering blue gown with the silver Louboutin sandals my mother gave me for my birthday. The dress is cut conservatively but slips and slides over my curves in a way that always makes me feel sexy.

The extra time is going to be so worth it when I see Zack's face. Although when I open the door at his knock, the shock is on me. Zack stands in the doorway wearing a black tuxedo that looks perfectly fitted. With his dark hair slicked back, I almost don't recognize him.

He raises his eyebrows when he sees my shock. "Pretty fancy for a mechanic, huh?"

I lick my lips appreciatively. "I'll say. Very impressive."

He holds out his arm and escorts me down the driveway.

"Where's your car?" I ask after we're on the way. He's driving Gabe's sleek black Audi R8 instead of his usual car.

"I figured it might be a bit much for the country club crowd. Disappointed?"

"You know it. I love that car."

"We had a new customer come in looking for some custom updates on a Venom GT."

He snickers as I almost break my neck swiveling in my seat. "Are you serious? Do you think they'd mind if I took pictures?"

"I'm sure he wouldn't but I'll ask." He chuckles at my excitement.

After hanging out with him and Gabe for so long, it's only natural that I fell in love with cars right along with them. Jim started teaching them about cars after he caught them trying to steal one of his. Luckily he took an interest in two father-less boys instead of turning them in to the cops.

By the time I met them, they were both already proficient mechanics. I remember plenty of weekends tagging along with them to the garage where Jim worked back then.

We pull up to the front of the club and one of the valets opens my door. I accept his hand to get out of the car without tripping over my dress. Zack meets me and together we walk through the entryway and into the ballroom. It's been decorated with tons of white roses, my mother's favorite flower.

As soon as we enter the room, I see my parents. My father is in a dove gray tuxedo and mom's dress is a deep violet that complements him. When she sees us, her lips tighten. She taps on my father's arm to get his attention and they move toward us.

"Hi, Mom. Dad. Happy Anniversary." I greet them both with a hug.

"That dress is very becoming, Josie." It's rare to get a compliment from my mother and the fact that she's making an effort to be pleasant is a relief.

"Thanks, Mom."

"Hi pumpkin. Have you been here long?" My father glances at Zack standing just behind me after he returns my hug.

A burble of laughter threatens to spring from my throat as I realize he probably had no idea I broke up with Perry. Very little penetrates through to him unless it's relevant to his business.

"We just arrived. Mom, Dad, you both remember Zack Marshall?"

"Zack. Of course. Of course." Dad recovers quickly from his befuddlement and shakes hands with Zack heartily enough.

My mother smiles tightly but doesn't offer her hand. "Hello again, Zachary."

"Lovely to see you, Mrs. Harlow. Happy anniversary."

Her demeanor softens at the sentiment. "Thank you so much."

Wow. I glance at Zack from the corner of my eye. He's really making an effort to be polite. My mother hasn't been this pleasant to him the entire time she's known him. As they move on to mingle with the other guests, I'm feeling cautiously optimistic. Maybe this won't be the disaster I feared.

Every year, Jamie and I are seated with my parents at the front table so I already know where to go. We weave our way between the tables toward the front and I stop every so often to say hello to people I recognize. I'm careful to introduce

Zack but not to linger too long. I don't want to use up his quota of social interaction so early in the night.

My grandparents are also seated at our table so I introduce them to Zack before sitting down. There's already champagne on the table and I take a healthy sip, hoping it will calm my nerves. The napkin on Jamie's seat is unfolded and I recognize Isabelle's wrap on the back of the chair next to me so I know they're here somewhere.

"Geez, you weren't kidding about this being boring."

When I look over at Zack in horror, he grins. "I'm kidding. Take a breath, sweetheart. You look like you're about to pass out."

I'm relieved that he seems to be so calm. A few people are staring, mainly friends of Perry's, but otherwise it's not so bad. The servers come around with salads and I ask for oil and vinegar.

"Thank you," Zack says when the server leaves.

"For what?"

"Asking for the oil and vinegar. Even though he should know my diet better than anyone, even Gabe forgets sometimes."

"Of course. To be honest, the way you eat has always inspired me to be healthier. I would have never known how much hidden sugar is in everything if I hadn't had a reason to think about it."

"Still, thank you. It's tiring sometimes to always be the person asking for something different."

After about ten minutes, Jamie and Isabelle appear with my parents right behind them. Jamie pulls out the chair next to me so Izzie can sit down. My father is on his other side. He gives me a look that makes me giggle. He's in for a night of hearing our father drone on about whatever case he's currently working on.

The oil and vinegar arrives then and we make meaningless conversation while we munch on our salads.

When the servers start bringing out the main course, it occurs to me that I ordered beef for Perry when I originally responded to the invitation. Then I immediately feel guilty for not remembering this earlier. Zack rarely eats red meat. Managing his diabetes is a delicate balance. Whenever we go out to eat, Zack usually goes to the bathroom after we order to give himself however much insulin he'll need for dinner. He usually sticks to chicken, fish and vegetables mainly.

I lean over to Zack and whisper, "You can have my chicken plate. The side is some kind of vegetable medley. I can find out what it is."

"That's fine. It's not a problem."

After I direct the server to give Zack my chicken plate, he excuses himself to go to the bathroom. He comes back five minutes later. He winks as he sits down. The steak is succulent and juicy and I'm soon too busy eating to worry anymore. Izzie leans over whispering the tidbits she's overhearing from the table behind her and Zack is having a spirited conversation with my Nana Harlow.

My father's mother is a bit irreverent anyway and the twinkle in her eye tells me she's enjoying having such an attentive neighbor. Although they seem to be having a pleasant conversation, Zack's smile is a little strained and he keeps tugging at his bowtie. I figure this has to be killing him.

After our plates are taken away, the dance floor starts to fill. Jamie stands and holds out a hand to a surprised Isabelle. She glances at me and then takes it. I turn to Zack.

"Do you want to dance?"

He looks relieved and we follow Izzie and Jamie to the dance floor. We find room amidst the swaying couples and he seems to relax for the first time since we've arrived.

"Is that better?"

"What do you mean?"

"You seemed really tense back there. I thought maybe getting away from the table would help."

"I'm not tense. I'm fine."

But I can tell he's lying. He can hide his emotions from everyone else but not from me. Not anymore.

"What's really wrong, Zack? Do you want to leave? We can. We've been here long enough."

He immediately looks chagrined. "Nothing's wrong. Sorry, I don't want to ruin this for you. I'm just not used to this kind of thing. And I'm trying not to step on your feet."

I pull him closer. "You don't seem to have any problem moving your body, Zack. In any way."

Finally a real smile appears. I rest my head on his shoulder. I was so worried about this earlier and all my fears seem so silly now. I showed up with Zack and the world didn't end. My parents weren't overly warm but they weren't outright rude either so that's probably about the best I can hope for.

When I open my eyes, Perry is right next to us, dancing with a tall skinny blonde. He looks just as surprised to see me. Or rather to see me in someone else's arms.

"Josie! Nice to see you." His eyes slide over to Zack. "Hello."

Zack's arm tenses around my waist. "Hey."

I straighten up. "Perry. What are you doing here?" He was originally supposed to escort me but after we broke up, I'd assumed that he wouldn't come.

He looks uncomfortable at the direct questioning. "I'm here with my parents."

I glance over my shoulder and see Mr. and Mrs. Staunchfield talking to my father. I sigh. In addition to doing business together, his father and mine have been golf buddies for years so I should have expected that he might be here anyway.

"Of course. How have you been?"

"Busy. My dad has been keeping us all in the office around the clock. Oh, I'm being rude. Josie, this is Blythe Wyndham. She's one of the new project managers we've just hired."

Blythe holds out her hand reluctantly. "Nice to meet you."

"Nice to meet you, too. This is my friend, Zack Marshall."

Blythe hangs on to Zack's hand a little longer than appropriate, something Perry doesn't seem to notice. He doesn't even seem to notice she's there at all.

"You look good, Jo." His voice lowers and even though it's a common thing to say, it comes across as incredibly familiar considering our history.

"Uh, thanks. You too." He's still staring at me and I can tell Zack is starting to get pissed off.

I imagine how this must look to him. Perry is tall, dark and handsome in a very clean-cut All-American kind of way just like Gabe. Basically the anti-Zack. No wonder he found it hard to believe me when I told him how I felt. Suddenly I want to be anywhere but here.

"Well, it was lovely to meet you, Blythe. I'll see you around, Perry."

Zack turns us in the other direction but over his shoulder I can see Perry still watching us.

Chapter Thirteen

Zack

Josie is quiet as we leave the dance floor. She follows as I head straight for the bar. I order a light beer and a glass of champagne for her. I'm almost afraid to speak because with the way I'm feeling anything I say will be either snarky or accusatory.

"Why is he even here?" I say, finally.

"His parents are close friends with mine."

"So he'll be at every family event then? *Great.*"

When Josie's shoulders curl inward, I immediately regret the sarcasm. I'm not sure why I'm suddenly so pissed when I knew she dated Perry for almost a year. Plus, she's the one who broke it off. It wasn't like she was dumped and is pining away for the guy.

I have the ultimate proof that she wasn't *that* close to him.

"Let's go back to the table. I don't want you to miss dessert."

She shrugs. "I don't care about that. We can say goodbye to everyone and then we can leave early."

Guilt makes me determined to put on a smile and be as fake as the rest of the people here. Jo has been on edge all night and I've tried not to embarrass her. She cares what these people think even if I can't figure out why.

I just want her to be happy.

We haven't been sitting for more than a minute when a shadow falls over my shoulder and I look up.

Perry is standing right behind us.

"Hello, Mr. and Mrs. Harlow. I wanted to make sure I got a chance to say Happy Anniversary before I left." He rounds the table to greet them. They both react like he's some kind of long-lost relative just returning home.

Oh for fucks sake.

Mrs. Harlow stands, her arms outstretched. "How sweet! Thank you, Perry. You're always so thoughtful!"

It's hard not to contrast her reaction to when I said the same thing earlier.

Then I hear, "Oh no. He's not her boyfriend! Josie has been running around with them since she was a kid. They're practically siblings! You know that."

I clench my jaw so hard I'm surprised I don't break a tooth. Josie stiffens beside me so I know she's heard it, too. She pushes her chair back and clutches her jeweled bag to her chest.

"We're going to leave. I'll see you guys at home." She hugs Isabelle and then leans over to say something to her brother.

Perry shakes hands with Josie's father. I can't hear what they're talking about from across the table but Jo has mentioned before that her parents only wanted her with Perry since their families have done business together.

"Of course you've been busy! Didn't you just win a major bid last week? It was all over the business news."

Josie's mother is practically simpering now and I can just hear her mentally tabulating how many millions Josie's missing out on by not snagging Perry while she could. If she only knew that my bank account is easily as big as any of theirs.

A grin breaks out on my face and Perry stutters in the middle of his sentence when he sees the look on my face. Probably wondering why I'm in such a good mood since he's the one her parents love.

"Y-Yes, we're working on that new development in Norfolk," he continues.

"Oh yes, one of our clients is involved. The zoning was a nightmare. Actually," Mr. Harlow glances across the table at me. "One of the investors is a Marshall. Finnigan Marshall, I believe. Any relation?" At his loud bellow the table quiets.

Perry scoffs. "I'm sure it's not. That's a pretty common last name."

Josie's hand lands on my arm. I turn my arm over and give her hand a comforting squeeze.

"Actually, Finn Marshall is my brother."

Mr. Harlow's eyebrows rise slowly and he looks at me with new interest. "I've heard great things about that project."

"It's been a bit of a bear but he mentioned that they've gotten past the zoning issues and are planning to expand. They'll be doing a few more luxury condo buildings and a mixed-use development as well. I believe that will be both condos and shops right in the heart of the city."

"Are you involved as well?"

Everyone at the table is suddenly interested in what I have to say. Even Josie's watching me with a look I don't recognize. Pride, maybe?

Perry on the other hand is seething.

I decide I might as well go for broke. I'm not one for bragging but after watching Josie's parents fawn all over him, I want them to know that I can take way better care of her than this puffed up blowhard.

"No, sir. My brother has asked me to invest but I have another cause in mind. When children in West Haven have diabetic complications, they're usually referred to New Haven's hospital since we don't have the resources to deal with them here. I've decided to endow a new pediatric wing of our hospital to address the issue."

Josie's grandmother speaks up. "That's a lovely idea. How generous of you."

"I have diabetes myself so it's a cause that's important to me. But honestly, Josie gave me the idea."

Josie's grip on my hand tightens. "Me? What did I do?"

"Earlier this evening, Josie knew to order oil and vinegar for me since I can't have the regular dressing on my salad. She also made sure to find out the meal options for me before dinner was served. It's difficult to manage this disease without family support."

I lift her hand to my lips. "Not everyone is lucky enough to have a Josie."

Next to us, Isabelle sighs. Even Mrs. Harlow is stunned into silence.

Glancing over at Josie, I'm surprised to find her eyes bright with unshed tears.

"*Zack.*" Her voice breaks a little.

Then she leans over and kisses me right there at the table.

***

The entire drive home I can feel Josie watching me. After kissing me in front of everyone, she promptly dragged me out of the ballroom. It was a good thing that we'd left our coats in the car because I don't think she would have even cared if we needed to stop at coat check.

I can feel her vibrating with anticipation from across the car.

As soon as I pull into her drive and put the car in park, she's over the seat. Her hands sink into my hair and her tongue is in my mouth while I struggle not to bang my knee on the steering wheel. She finally gets over the center console and settles in my lap, straddling me. She arches and then my lips are on her throat.

"Zack, I want you."

Her voice is throaty in the way I've come to recognize as her *fuck me now* voice.

"Josie. The house. Now."

I'm so turned on I can barely form complete sentences. But somehow I get the door open and we almost fall out onto the pavement.

She's all over me as we walk-stumble up the drive. It takes her a few minutes to get out her keys and get the door open. Then I pick her up and carry her up the stairs. She turns her back to me and I carefully pull down the zipper on the back of her gown, kissing the creamy skin revealed. It falls in a heap around her ankles and she steps out of it.

My heart stops for a moment at my first sight of Josie in a black strapless bra, black thong and those sky-high fuck me heels.

"You are everything."

I'm not sure if she really understands what I mean when I say that but she launches herself at me, tearing at my shirt. She makes a sound of frustration when she can't get it off. I laugh at her little growl and pull off my jacket and then undo the buttons of the shirt.

"These damn buttons are keeping me from the good stuff," she mutters before her lips land on my bare chest.

The sound I make shocks even me. But last time I was focused completely on Josie. This is the first time I've felt her lips on my bare skin like this and the sensation is sublime.

She tugs at my waistband and I quickly get out of my pants and boxers. Her mouth falls open when my erection pops free, almost hitting her in the face. Her hand grips me at the base, much more firmly than I would have expected.

"*Shit.* Stroke me, just like that," I whisper harshly.

My control is stretched thin by her uncharacteristic boldness.

Her touch is hesitant at first but she quickly catches a rhythm. She puts one hand in the middle of my chest and forces me to walk backwards. The back of my thighs hit the bed and Josie drops to her knees. I'm thinking that she'll be nervous or need direction but before I can even think, her lips are wrapped around me.

My head falls back and I let out a deep moan as I watch the head of my cock disappear into her mouth and then reappear shiny and wet. The visual is almost as powerful as the physical sensations.

She doesn't try to take it deep but just licks delicately like it's a treat she's tasting. My hands grip the comforter to keep from tangling in her hair and forcing her head down. Her untutored but enthusiastic tongue has me hovering on the edge of insanity already.

My dick pops out of her mouth and she glances up at me, her eyes wide with curiosity and desire.

"Is this the right way?"

"Anything you want to do is right, sweetheart. Just take as much as you can."

She seems to take that as a challenge, sweeping her hair over her shoulder before she takes it all the way to the back of her throat. The look on her face, the sounds she's making, the way she holds me, all tell me that she's into it. Her arousal feeds mine until we're moving together in perfect harmony, my hips lifting as she comes down.

I can't take any more.

When I pull back, she makes a soft sound of disgruntlement but then she's laughing when I scoop her up in my arms. I place her in the middle of the bed, coming down on top of her. We both sigh at the pleasurable sensation of skin sliding over skin. Her arms curl around my neck and I revel in being wrapped up in her embrace.

I've always been a solitary person, needing nothing and no one to survive. It always seemed easier that way.

There's no disappointment if you never expect anything.

It's a scary thing to find myself at home in her arms when I never thought I needed that.

She reaches over to her nightstand and pulls out a box of condoms.

"I got these today on the way home."

It introduces a moment of levity as I imagine her going into the store, blushing while she bought these.

"Thank you for being a good Girl Scout sweetheart because I don't want to get up and search for mine."

Her legs tighten behind my back and I groan as her hot, wet heat presses against my stomach.

"I don't want you going anywhere either," she murmurs in that throaty voice.

She laughs as I fumble the condom open, my eagerness obvious. Then her giggles are cut off by her long intake of breath as I push inside. She's still so tight and it's a struggle to go slow.

"Zack, I need you." She pulls on my shoulders, trying to force me to go faster.

"Slowly, sweetheart."

I kiss her gently, rocking my hips slowly, gaining an inch at a time. When she lifts her hips again, I slide home and we both cry out.

Her nails bite into my back and her neck arches as she tries to get me deeper. Her tight muscles squeeze me so hard that I can tell she's already close and after just a few short strokes, she's coming. Tears slide down her cheeks as she gives herself over to the pleasure, sobbing and cursing as her orgasm rolls through her.

I love it. It's so fucking sexy to watch her lose control of herself.

Seeing the pleasure on her face and hearing her helpless little cries has me right behind her, my hips moving faster until I can't take it any more and let go.

Afterward we lay entwined, completely destroyed by the intensity of our lovemaking. I don't raise my head to look at her yet, wanting a few more moments to pretend I haven't just been irrevocably changed.

Looking in the mirror when I was dressing for the party, I didn't even recognize myself. With my hair grown in and my tats covered, it was like someone else had climbed into my skin.

Worrying about what people think is alien to me but suddenly I'm changing my hair, my clothes and my demeanor to fit into her world. I hate that I've so easily thrown aside what I believe to appease others but I can't deny I would do the same thing again.

The fact is, I would compromise every part of myself to make Josie happy and it scares the hell out of me.

—————

Finally I roll over and pull Josie on top of me. Her breathing slows down and after a few minutes I assume she's gone to sleep. I'm almost asleep myself when her voice jerks me back to attention.

"I know you heard what my mother said tonight." She lifts her head from my chest to look at me. "I'm sorry you had to hear that."

"She's right. I'm not your boyfriend."

"You're angry."

She cups my cheeks and holds my face still so I can't avoid her eyes.

"Why are you mad? Did you want me to correct her? Zack, you're the one who said we have to keep our relationship a secret."

She's right. I'm the one who insisted on drawing these lines.

I'm tripping over my own rules because I've seen how much better life is with her in it.

Now that I know how deep my need for her runs, I'm terrified of what will happen if I lose her. It's not her fault that I'm so torn up.

"I'm not angry with you, Jo. It was just... everything tonight was so wrong. I felt like a fraud wearing that stupid tux and listening to your mother talking about what a perfect catch your ex is. He's everything she's ever wanted for you."

"I should have stopped her. Standing up to her is difficult for me but that's my problem not yours. I don't care if she wants me to be with Perry. I want to be with *you*."

"She's not going to be the only one thinking those things and you do deserve the best, Jo. But I'm a blue-collar kind of guy. That's never going to change."

"And I would never ask you to," she assures me.

"But *they* will. They'll expect a guy who can fit into your world. I can clean up nice for an evening but that's not who I am. I can't be that guy as much as I want to be."

"You really think I care about all that? About diamonds and parties and the social scene? I couldn't possibly care any less about that stuff."

"I know."

The worst part is that I *do* know. Josie truly doesn't care about the superficial. She's so genuine and real.

She sits up slightly so she can see my face. "What do you think is going to happen down the line? That I'll change my mind about us?"

I can't respond and admit that she's just stated my worst fear. But her tremulous smile as she kisses me again tells me that as always, she knows.

"I'm not changing my mind. You're just going to have to get used to the idea of me loving you."

Her emotions shine from her eyes like a beacon. Even if she'd never told me before, I'd know she loves me just by looking at her. It makes me feel like a caveman who wants to beat his chest and claim her and also scared as hell.

"You're telling me you love me. I don't know if I have that in me. Not the way you need me to. You deserve so much better than that."

Her ex probably had no problem telling her he loved her whether he meant it or not. But I can never lie to Josie even if it means I get to keep her special smiles and love all to myself.

"I'm going to go."

"Don't leave mad. I won't be able to sleep knowing we're angry with each other."

"When we started this, I promised I would be careful with you."

"You have been. I couldn't imagine a better or more considerate lover than you've been. I hate to think of how it would have been if I'd tried to do this with anyone else. You would *never* hurt me."

Her faith in me makes my inadequacy all the more obvious.

"Don't you see? I'm already hurting you."

"You're only hurting me if you run away."

I nod and then pull her into the cradle of my arms. Cuddling with her has become one of my favorite things in a very short time. I didn't get nearly enough time to enjoy having her warm, curvy body in my arms last time before we were interrupted.

"Go to sleep, sweetheart. I promise I won't leave until you fall asleep."

She stretches against me trying to get comfortable. Then she tucks her hand under my stomach and rests her head on my arm. She blinks sleepily a few times, then yawns. Eventually she ends her fight to stay awake and I watch as she sleeps trustingly in my arms.

If someone had told me a few weeks ago that I would be wearing tuxedos and covering my tattoos for a girl, I wouldn't have believed it. But here I am and I can't deny that I'd do it all over again if I had to.

This entire time I've been warning Josie about not equating sex with love but it turns out she's not the one in danger.

I was so busy warning her that sex would change things that I never considered it might change *me*.

There's no denying I *have* changed. And I kind of like it.

But what happens when she meets someone who fits better into her world? A guy who doesn't come up with an idea to help others to impress her parents but just because he's a nice guy?

I can put on a performance but what happens when she pulls back the curtain and discovers it's all a show?

Chapter Fourteen

Josie

Something hits me in the side and I startle awake. My eyes dart around, trying to figure out what woke me. The dark in the room is broken only by the sliver of moonlight coming in between the curtains. It's quiet and still. Then I turn over and see Zack.

He didn't leave.

I watch his chest rise and fall slowly. He must have pulled the sheet over us at some point because all I can see is his naked chest. He's so beautiful like this and without his usual scowl he looks younger. Unburdened somehow. Kind of like how he looked when we first met.

Propping myself up on one arm, I watch him sleep, thrilled

with the opportunity to observe him while he's unaware. No one else gets to see him like this but me. My heart beats a little faster just looking at this face I love so much.

I could look at this every day and never get tired of it.

That gives me an idea.

Carefully I climb out of bed, hoping my movements won't wake him. Our clothes are still scattered all over the floor from our mad scramble to get in bed earlier. My camera is sitting on my desk so I turn it on and then open the curtains slightly to let in more of the moonlight.

Zack doesn't stir as I take pictures of him from every angle. For the first time in years I'm given license to do what I want.

Stare at him.

Through the lens you can see things you'd otherwise miss. He's such an interesting puzzle to look at. All hard angles and lines from his cheekbones to the lean muscles in his chest but then he has the most enticing spots that show a hint of vulnerability.

The way his hair curls right behind his ears, the long lashes and elegant fingers that I know can work magic on the most sensitive parts of my body.

Just thinking about what he can do with those beautiful fingers sends a warm flush of heat straight between my thighs.

Zack grunts and then one eye opens. His lazy smile is so adorable I take a picture of that, too.

"What are you doing, sweetheart?"

"Taking pictures of the hot, naked man in my bed."

He reaches out and grabs me around the waist, pulling me down on top of him. "Take pictures of us together."

I take a photo while straddling him and then the camera slips out of my fingers when he lifts his hips, grinding against me.

Maybe I could withstand it if I wasn't completely nude but his hand lands on my ass, rocking me into him and I'm done. I want him inside me. I want that thick length stretching and pounding into me, bringing me pleasure that I didn't even know existed.

This time I take the initiative, reaching over him to grab a condom from the nightstand. I'm not really sure how to put it on but he takes it from me and together we roll it down his shaft. By the time we get to the wide base, Zack is panting and so am I.

"Ride me, baby. Take me in."

He guides my hips in place and then I sink down, inch by inch. Even after making love several times, it's such a tight, delicious fit. I lean forward, my hands on his chest so I can control the angle. Before long he's sliding into me with ease because I'm so wet, so hot for him.

He lifts his hips to get deeper and hits that spot inside that makes me crazy.

"I love this Zack. I love it all."

His eyes flare and his fingers tighten around my waist. I hope he can hear what I'm really saying. That I don't just love the sex.

I love *him*.

The friction is unbearable and before long we're both moaning, straining against each other as the tension builds. It feels like a storm gathering inside me and when he reaches between us to stroke my clit in time with the rhythm of each harsh thrust, I explode.

My fists fall against my thighs as I ride out wave after wave of blistering pleasure and when Zack stiffens beneath me, I know he feels it, too.

Afterward, he gathers me close and wraps his arms around me. Neither of us speak. The things I'm feeling are too complicated for words. My love for him is tempered by my fear of overwhelming him and pushing him away.

He's already feeling pressure, his words earlier prove that. He thinks I want him to change, to conform, to fit the image that would gain my parents' approval. When all I really want is the one thing I can't ask for.

For him to realize he loves me just as much as I love him.

After I finally fall asleep again, my dreams are tormented. I'm chasing Zack and he's always just out of reach. He's wearing his tuxedo but for some reason when I look down at my own clothes, I'm wearing my paint-splattered coveralls.

I wake up confused and feeling like I didn't get any rest at all. Then I roll over and see the empty space next to me. Zack left in the middle of the night.

Suddenly I wonder if my dreams weren't a warning.

If I keep chasing Zack, there's a chance he'll run away and won't come back.

———

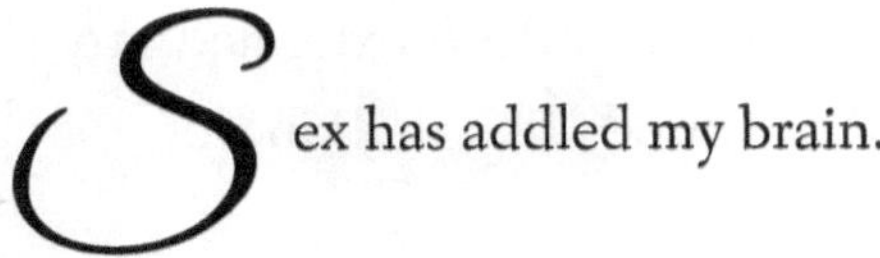

Sex has addled my brain.

Zack has been coming over every evening to spend time with me for the past week, which has worked out since we've had the house to ourselves a lot.

Izzie has been going out with her friends and I'm not sure what's up with Jamie. He's been weird and strangely grumpy lately, too. But all the time alone has meant lots of opportunities to indulge in my new favorite activity. We've been all over this house in every position and there are a few days where I was surprised I could walk properly afterward.

All the sex has truly addled my brain.

That's the only reason I can think of why it takes me so long to realize something is wrong with Zack.

He comes over on Friday after work and the first thing I notice are the dark circles under his eyes. I lead him to the couch and sit next to him. He leans his head back against the cushion and closes his eyes.

"You look tired, babe. Come on. We can take a little nap." I grab his hand and he allows me to pull him to his feet.

I lead him upstairs to my room and he stretches out on the bed while I sit in my desk chair. His deep extended groan when his head hits the pillow sounds like the kind of noise he'd make during sex.

"Wow, you're really exhausted. You're welcome to just sleep over if you want. Then you won't have to get up later and drive home."

I hope my eagerness isn't completely obvious. I want to sleep wrapped up in his embrace and wake up the same way.

But so far, he never stays with me.

He doesn't look at me as he says, "Don't worry. I'll be fine in about an hour. I need to get home anyway. Tank and Finn were at the house visiting Gabe when I left."

I ignore the tickle of disappointment at how he always manages to avoid any talk of sleeping over.

"What are they up to?"

"Tank's getting married and asked Gabe for help with the vows. He said the only thing he could think of to say was '*If I'm in a coma, I trust her not to pull the plug.*' I thought that was pretty good."

I laugh. "That's great. I hope they left that in."

"Gabe came up with some flowery shit that's basically a nicer way of saying the same thing."

He's quiet for a minute then says, "When I came home that night after the anniversary party, Gabe asked where I was."

I sit up immediately. No wonder he's being so weird.

"What did you tell him?"

"The truth. Sort of. I told him I escorted you to the party and then fell asleep here afterward."

"Well, that's good. I think you're being overly cautious. Yes, it'll be awkward when we first tell everyone, especially your moms, but it's no big deal."

He snorts. "You didn't see his face. This is going to turn into an entire cluster of fucks if we're not careful."

"I hope not. I would never want to come between you guys. You're family. Jamie and I haven't been as close as I'd like but we're changing that. Having those bonds is so important."

Zack makes a sound of agreement but the effort seems to take a lot out of him. His skin looks so pale and there's a fine sheen of sweat on his brow.

"Are you okay, Zack?"

He rolls over. "Yeah, I'm just tired. Sorry, I'm not too entertaining today."

"Don't worry about ... that." I'm laughing and blushing at the same time when I realize what he's referring to. "I don't need to be *entertained* right now. I just want to make sure you're okay."

"It's just stress."

If this is stress, then I'm going to be a basket case if he ever gets truly sick. He pats the bed next to him and I climb over his legs and stretch out.

"Anything I can help with?"

He shakes his head. "Stress tends to send my blood sugar levels through the roof. I just need to relax."

"Close your eyes."

He closes them obediently and I stroke his hair back from his face gently. He lets out a deep sigh. Soon his breathing is steady and even. After about ten minutes, he opens his eyes again.

"My blood monitor is in the car. Can you get it?"

"Actually, I have one here. I bought it just in case you might need it."

I get up and walk into the bathroom across the hall from my room. The first aid kit and the blood monitor I bought are below the sink. I bring it back to him and he inspects the packaging.

As he's opening it, I notice his hands are shaking slightly. It's not fun to prick yourself on any given day but trying to do it when your hands aren't steady sounds like torture.

"Do you want me to do it for you?"

His eyes lift to mine. "You don't have to do that. That's a lot to ask."

"Nothing is too much to ask. I want to help you."

He stares at me so long I wonder if he thinks it's weird that I even asked that.

"I guess that means you wouldn't pull the plug on me, then."

Even though he's joking, there's a question in his eyes I can't leave unanswered.

"I would do anything for you, Zack."

"I know," he replies softly.

His eyes stay on me the whole time as I prick his finger and press it against the test strip. I slide the strip into the machine. After it beeps, I show him the readout.

"It's a little high still but not as bad as it was," he says.

My audible sigh of relief coaxes a chuckle out of Zack. I would have *really* hated to have to prick his finger a second time.

"In sickness and in health," he murmurs.

I glance at him in shock but his eyes are closed. After a few minutes, his breathing evens out.

He's asleep.

____

When Zack calls the next day, he's quieter than usual. I wonder if I've turned him off by being too sentimental. Just because I've loved him forever doesn't mean he's going to be in the same place emotionally right away.

He has a right to want to take things slow. Sleeping over is a big deal and I don't want to push him into it or make him feel obligated to do it. It should be something that happens naturally.

I have to remind myself that everyone doesn't live with their heart on their sleeve like I do.

"Give the guy a chance to catch up, Josie," I mumble to myself.

"Huh?" Isabelle looks over at me from the kitchen table where she's sitting with her coffee and a magazine.

"Nothing."

"What?" Zack's voice in my ear reminds me that he's still there.

"Sorry, I was talking to Izzie. What did you say?"

"I just asked if you changed your mind about coming tonight?"

"Coming where?"

"The opening of Sasha's jazz lounge is tonight. It's supposed to be quite a party."

"That's *tonight*?" I freeze.

After marking it on my calendar, I promptly forgot all about it. Luckily I didn't plan anything else for tonight so it's okay.

I move into the living room, away from Izzie's curious ears. She's been very respectful of my time with Zack so far, probably because she can tell how much it means to me. But that doesn't mean she won't jump on anything juicy she overhears. We're still figuring out things between us and I'm not ready to talk about it with anyone else yet.

"What time are we going?" I ask once I'm out of her earshot.

"That's the thing. We can't show up together. Everyone will see us."

Now that's annoying. Even though I understand his reasoning behind keeping things to ourselves, I'm tired of the secrecy and sneaking around. There's no reason we should be made to feel like we're doing something wrong when we're not.

Then I imagine everyone I know talking about the fact that I'm sleeping with Zack. And what if it doesn't work out? Then I'll be not only heartbroken but humiliated as I have to deal with all the questions. Just the thought makes my cheeks burn.

Maybe I'm not quite as ready to go public as I think I am.

"Does that mean I won't get to see you at all tonight?"

I stick out my bottom lip in a pout even though he can't see me. He growls and the sound turns me on even over the phone.

"Hell, no. I'm coming home with you after."

That makes me feel better.

"Okay, see you then."

I slip my cellphone into my pocket and walk back into the kitchen to grab a yogurt from the refrigerator. Izzie is staring into space looking kind of glum.

"You want to come with me to the opening of a jazz lounge tonight?"

That perks her right up. "Sounds fun! I'd love to come. I've missed hanging out with you."

I instantly feel guilty. I've been so wrapped up in Zack that I've pretty much checked out of every other area of my life.

"Well, this is right up your alley. Boys, booze and booty-shaking."

She smiles but it doesn't quite reach her eyes. "Is that what you think of me? That I'm only out for a good time?"

I sit across from her and grasp her hand on top of the table. "Of course not. I didn't mean it that way."

"It's no big deal. I'm just sensitive today. Hormonal."

She rolls her eyes. But the tension doesn't leave her mouth and she can't quite meet my eyes.

"Izzie, is everything okay?"

Under my scrutiny she straightens her shoulders.

"Sure. Give me an hour and I'll be ready to go. Nothing gets between me and a party."

She squeezes my hand and then gets up to put her coffee cup in the sink. As she walks away, I wonder at the strange change in her demeanor.

Maybe I'm not the only one keeping secrets lately.

Chapter Fifteen

Zack

Later that evening, I stand naked in front of the mirror in my bathroom. What's reflected back is mainly the same as what I've been staring at my whole life. Except for one critical difference.

This guy is clearly in love.

My clippers feel heavy in my hand. This is the longest I've gone without shaving my head in years. The new look doesn't bother me as much as I would have thought it would.

However, the reason I did it does.

I've been changing who I am for her and that's not how I want to live. Pretending to fit in her world by compromising every aspect of my self.

What will I have to change next? That's what worries me the most. Not knowing where it ends.

I love Josie enough to give her the real me. And I have to trust her enough to want me exactly as I am.

The buzz of the clippers soothes me as I take all the hair off on both sides. Then I get out my razor. When I'm done, the lightning bolts tattooed on either side of my scalp are once again visible. I smile at the familiar image in the mirror.

I'm back.

"Zack, are you coming with me?"

I startle at Gabe's loud voice right outside the door.

"No, I'll meet you there," I yell back.

Footsteps sound on the stairs and then the front door closes. Sasha left earlier in the day to supervise last minute details. Gabe told me that she had a bad experience on a reality show that almost put her off performing entirely. I rarely watch television so I had no idea.

Apparently tonight she'll be performing a new song. Her excitement is infectious and I'm happy to see her doing what she's passionate about.

When I arrive at *The Lounge*, all the parking on both sides of the street is taken. I park a few streets over and walk back, raising the collar on my leather jacket to block the wind. Glancing around at the dark streets, I wonder if Josie has arrived yet. I hate thinking of her walking out here alone.

I give my name to the guy at the door and then enter the throng of dancing people. The decor is old-school speakeasy and gives me a decadent Prohibition-era vibe. My eyes skim over the people dancing around me until I locate Tank on the other side of the room. Our oldest brother is six foot five easily and hard to miss even in a crowded room.

When I reach him, I see he's standing with Finn and our youngest brother, Luke. I bump fists with the guys and I give Tank's fiancée, Emma, a quick hug.

I look at Finn. "Where's Rissa?"

He smiles at the sound of her name. "She had a job she couldn't get out of. But she'll be here a little later."

The crowd goes wild when Sasha steps on stage and performs her new song. I glance around again, looking for Josie. Where the hell is she? It's already dark outside and the later it gets, the more deserted the streets will be.

I glance at my phone. Maybe I should call and find out where she is. I could always go meet her outside and walk her in.

I'm so busy thinking about Jo that I don't even notice Sasha's finished performing until the crowd goes crazy again.

I circle the room once, thinking maybe Jo is at the bar or on the dance floor. I'm getting frustrated when slim arms encircle me from behind. Then I hear a throaty voice I'd know anywhere.

"Hey sexy, can I get your number?"

I laugh and then turn around. She's dressed in all black and wearing this red gloss that makes her lips look wet. My heart skips a beat when I take in the skintight black jeans and her skimpy black tank top.

I'm supposed to pretend that I don't want her and she dresses like this?

She's trying to kill me.

"I was just about to call you. Did you drive?"

"No, I caught a ride with Isabelle. Know anyone who wouldn't mind giving me a ride home?"

She winks and then saunters off. I'm two seconds from following when someone taps me on the shoulder. I turn to see Gabe and Sasha.

"You're finally here!" Sasha pulls me into a hug.

I can tell she's had a few drinks because she's extremely affectionate when she's tipsy. I smirk at Gabe over her shoulder.

He immediately pulls her out of my arms. "Get your own."

Working on it, I think.

"Did you come by yourself?" Gabe asks.

"Yeah. Why wouldn't I?"

He gives me a strange look. "Just wondering. I thought I saw you talking to someone earlier."

Shit. He probably saw Josie grab me but wasn't close enough to be able to tell who it was.

"Where is Josie? I hope she comes. She's so much fun. Isn't she so much fun, Zack?"

Sasha is staring at me in a way that makes me wonder what she knows. Just because Gabe couldn't see who I was talking to earlier doesn't mean she didn't.

"Yeah, I guess."

"Ooh! I just remembered. I'm giving out prizes. Can you get them from the storage closet for me? It's a big green box." Sasha points to a door on the other side of the room, in the corridor with the bathrooms.

"Sure. No problem." I walk away, happy for the excuse to cross the room and look for Josie.

Someone coming out of one of the bathrooms brushes past me as I walk down the corridor. I turn the handle and enter the room. Josie turns around. The door closes behind me and the noise from the club is immediately silenced.

"Wow, this must be soundproofed."

She grins and then turns back around, reaching for something on one of the shelves.

"What are you doing in here? Miss me, already?"

"I'm getting something for Sasha. What are *you* doing in here?"

She whips around, her eyes wide. "I'm getting something for her, too. Oh, she better not have!"

She reaches for the door handle behind me and tugs. Then tugs again.

"I can't believe her!"

"What's wrong with the door? I just opened it."

Josie leans one hand on the back of the door and sighs. "There's nothing wrong with it. It's just locked."

I tug at the handle, too.

"Still locked." She raises her eyebrows at me.

"I was just checking, brat. Why the hell would Sasha lock us in her storage closet?"

Josie throws up her hands. "Because she knows how I feel about you. I had to tell her because she was worried I was after Gabe."

"*Christ*. If she knows, how long before she tells him?"

"She's known for a long time and hasn't said anything so I don't think she will. That won't stop her from playing match-maker though."

Suddenly the whole situation strikes me as funny. Josie gives me an annoyed look when I burst out laughing.

"This isn't funny!"

"Yes, it kind of is. Sasha thinks she's helping and really has no idea that her plan could end up blowing our whole cover."

After a few minutes, Josie tries the door again. Then she bangs on it. Considering how loud the music is, neither of us is surprised when no one comes to our aid.

"Maybe we should just tell everyone. This is crazy!"

"You know how protective Gabe is over you. He'll go ballistic and probably hurt himself trying to take me out."

She curls her arms around my neck in that way I love. "We can't have that. I don't want him messing up my merchandise. I need you in top form tonight."

"That's not the point. And for the record, I can take him *any* day of the week. Gabe fights like a pussy."

She laughs. "Of course you can. I know better than to insult the male ego. I just don't ever want to come between you two."

"Gabe isn't exactly rational where you're concerned. He thinks of you as this helpless princess in a tower."

"And you don't think of me as a princess, huh?"

"I do. I think of you as the sexy ass princess who is smart enough to get *herself* out of the damn tower."

I bend my head and kiss her gently. Then not so gently. She whimpers when I bite her neck. Then pulls out her phone.

"This princess is calling for backup. Izzie or somebody has to let us out of this damn closet so I can take you home!"

———

Once Isabelle liberates us from the closet, I say goodbye to Tank, Finn and Luke. Gabe and Sasha are nowhere to be found.

Probably hiding from us.

I chuckle when I think of Sasha's antics. It's a good thing she's in favor of our relationship but I will definitely have to let her know her matchmaking isn't needed.

When we park in front of Izzie's house, it's completely dark. I follow Josie inside and she immediately starts stripping off her clubbing outfit. The tank top lands on the floor and then I watch with interest as she shimmies her hips to get out of the tight jeans. Her black thong bisects her plump cheeks, emphasizing the perfect heart shape of her ass.

The view is almost enough to stop my heart.

She glances over her shoulder at me. "You like?"

"Oh sweetheart, there's no like here. Only love."

I don't miss the wistful look on her face at my words. She's been so patient and understanding while I figured things out. I want her to know how I feel. That I'm in this thing with her one hundred percent.

"I love everything about you, Jo." I whisper it against her shoulder before kissing right behind her ear.

She shudders beneath my hands, arching against me as I push down the sides of the flimsy thong so she can step out of it. When she straightens, I cup her heavy breasts.

"I love your breasts. How they fill my hands and how sensitive they are." I thumb her nipples and she cries out.

My hands trail down her stomach and dip into the indentation of her belly button.

"I love how soft you are. And how ticklish," I add when she giggles at the touch.

Then I'm delving between her thighs and her giggles stop.

"And I love hearing you scream for me. Nothing in the world like it."

As I curl my fingers into her wet heat, she whimpers, her head falling back onto my shoulder. I press deeper, searching for the right spot. She really does scream then, shaking and crying as I rub her to orgasm.

Before she even catches her breath, I have her in my arms. I settle her on the bed, then quickly put on a condom. Then I come down on top of her, holding myself up on one arm.

I want to see her face this time when I tell her I love her.

And I want her to see mine so she can see how much I mean it.

"I love you. In every way."

"*Zack*." Her eyes fill with tears and then widen as I thrust inside her.

Her fingers curl around my forearm as if she's expecting me to set a fast pace. But I move slowly, holding myself deep at the end of every stroke. I want her to feel me tomorrow and every day after that.

I want her to know that I'm home.

When we come, it's together, on a sweet rolling wave of heat. Her lashes flutter and her mouth falls open as she gasps her way through it.

I kiss her sweet lips just because I can. Because I can't get enough and never will.

After a few minutes, I catch my breath and raise my head to look at Jo. Her eyes are open and locked on my face. There's so much in her eyes, love, lust, happiness and then ... wariness.

She pushes against my shoulder gently until I let her up.

"I'm going to take a shower. It's late so I guess I'll say goodbye now."

She kisses me once and then again. Then she walks into the bathroom across the hall and closes the door behind her.

I'm left feeling like I'm out in the cold.

I pick up my shirt from the floor but don't put it on. Then I glance over at the bathroom door again. It sucked hiding our relationship from all our friends tonight. Not just because I can see that the secrecy hurts Jo but also because I want to tell everyone, too. I wanted to tell every single guy that was watching Josie's curvy body on the dance floor tonight that she's mine.

I want the right to be by her side all the time. Every night.

I don't want to leave.

When I enter the bathroom, Josie pauses in the act of brushing her teeth. She grabs the glass on the counter and then rinses her mouth.

"Did you forget something?"

I drop the shirt I'm still holding on the floor.

"Yeah, I did. *You.* I don't want to sleep without you. So, I'm staying over if you don't mind."

The most dazzling smile crosses her face. "Really?"

It's amazing how such a simple thing can bring her so much joy. But it shows me I've made the right choice in trusting her. In loving her. I don't even want to think about how much time I wasted worrying about all the wrong things. Time that we could have been together.

The best thing that ever happened to me was right there all along.

"I love you, Jo."

Her face crumples slightly and then she's in my arms. "I thought you were just saying that in the heat of the moment."

"I said it because I mean it. I love you."

There's a hiccup. Then a soft sob. *"Say it again, please."*

I laugh and bury my face in her hair. "I love you, sweetheart. I'll say it a thousand times from now on so you'll never forget."

When she raises her head, her eyes are shiny with tears. "I don't think I'll ever forget this moment."

Overcome, I lift her in my arms and spin her around until she's giggling. I wish I'd thought to do this in a more romantic setting but either way, I'm pretty sure I'll never forget it either.

After a long leisurely shower, we dry off sharing Jo's towel. I wrap it around my waist loosely while Jo just scampers across the hall, naked.

"I'll definitely be buying us our own place," I mutter.

Josie grins at me and raises her camera. She takes several pictures before I realize what she's doing.

"Will you say it again?"

For a moment, I'm not sure what she means. She waits patiently though until I figure it out.

"I love you, Josephine Harlow."

She snaps a picture of me just like that, naked save for the towel around my waist and the love in my eyes.

"I love you too, Zack Marshall."

Chapter Sixteen

Zack

The next morning, I wake up disoriented and uncomfortable. Even though I loved having Josie wrapped around me last night, I'm not used to sleeping in someone else's bed. Her mattress is firmer than mine and she's a bit of a cover hog. This is going to take some adjustment.

Then I realize the reason I woke up was because I felt someone's eyes on me. Isabelle is standing right next to the bed sipping nonchalantly from her coffee mug.

And I'm stark naked.

"Can I help you?" I grab the sheet and yank it over me.

The action wakes Josie, who sits straight up, her hair flying around her head. She's just as naked as I am.

"What is it? What's happening?" she mumbles.

I hold the sheet over her as well. "We have company."

When she sees Isabelle standing next to the bed, she clutches the sheet to her chest.

"Izzie! What are you doing? I'm naked! And Zack is naked!"

"I noticed," Isabelle drawls. "I knocked but no one answered."

"That doesn't mean come in!" Josie points out.

Izzie makes a face. "I wouldn't have but you've got company downstairs. Very insistent company."

"Why would anyone be here now?" Jo glances at the clock on her dresser. "It's not even ten o'clock in the morning."

"You're the early riser," Isabelle points out. "Gabe knows you rarely sleep in. I'll go tell him you're coming down."

"Gabe's here?" We ask in unison but Isabelle is already walking away.

Josie's eyes meet mine. "What are we going to do?"

"Get dressed." I throw back the sheet and put on the clothes I wore last night.

Josie pulls on a pair of sweatpants and a tank top. She winds her hair around her hand into a bun. "I feel like this looks kind of bad even though I shouldn't feel that way at all."

I don't say anything. I have a feeling it's about to be *really* bad but I'm hoping that I can get Gabe to neutral territory before he goes nuclear. His issue is with me not with Josie. Not really, anyway.

She opens her bedroom door and then jumps back. Gabe and Sasha are in the hallway.

"There you are! Since when do you sleep in?" I hear Gabe say before pulling Josie into a hug. "And what's up with Izzie? She was being really weird."

Then he notices me standing behind her.

"Zack, what are you–"

His eyes slide over to Josie, taking in the wild hair and the slight stubble burn on her neck. I know he doesn't miss a single detail. Sasha holds out her arms to me for a hug. I accept it gratefully.

"We came by to tell you guys some great news. We're engaged!" She holds out her left hand to display a massive diamond ring.

Josie hugs her and they do the squealing thing women do when they're excited.

Gabe is still watching me. The only thing moving on him is the muscle in his jaw. "So, how long has this been going on?"

Josie and Sasha get quiet.

Sasha finally laughs. "Gabe, it's none of our business. But since we're talking about it, I'm glad my matchmaking worked last night."

Gabe looks at her. *"You knew about this?"*

Sasha glances between us, uncertainly. "Um, yeah. I think anyone with eyes knew about this."

I can tell Gabe is about two seconds from losing his shit.

I kiss Josie on the forehead. "I need to talk to my brother. You were going to make pancakes, right?"

Gabe watches the interaction, glowering. I can practically feel the fire on the back of my neck.

She looks back and forth between the two of us nervously. I can tell she doesn't want to leave but finally, she nods her head.

"Okay. I'll go make breakfast. Sasha, do you mind?"

The girls leave, pulling the door closed behind them. When I turn around Gabe is staring at the bed. The covers are a mess and my shoes are right next to the bed on my side.

The thought catches me by surprise. My side?

But I realize that whenever we're in her bed, I always take the left side. A few months ago this level of familiarity would have freaked me out. But with Jo? It seems so natural.

Of course I have a side. Of course my shoes are under her bed. I belong here. It all just feels so right.

Gabe walks over to Josie's desk. There's an entire stack of pictures on top. I already know they're all of me. He flips through them, his movements more agitated every second.

"*Are you kidding me?* I asked you to convince her it was a bad idea. Not volunteer yourself as fucking tribute!" His face twists into a sneer as he drops the pictures back onto the desk. "I guess you saw your opening and took it, huh?"

It's a struggle not to lash out. But both of us being angry won't make this situation any easier.

"That's not how it went down."

He shakes his head. "I know exactly how it went down. You waited until the first moment she was vulnerable to take what you wanted."

I freeze in place. It's hard work to control my breathing because it feels like I'm almost hyperventilating.

"What the hell are you talking about?"

"You think I'm blind, Zack? I've seen the way you've been looking at her lately."

My skin boils under the heat of his censure, shame lighting me up from within. All this time I thought I'd hidden my little obsession for Jo from everyone.

Turns out I was about as covert as a freaking billboard.

"We're adults, Gabe. It's none of your business."

"The two of you don't even get along! She's confused! It hasn't even been a month since she broke up with her boyfriend. She doesn't know what she wants right now."

"That's unfair. She knows exactly what she wants. And it's me."

"You know what, I'm done."

The look of disgust on his face almost takes me to my knees. Growing up we got our fair share of those looks from others but we always had each other. My brother was my partner in crime, my confidante and my best friend.

I never thought he would look at me like I'm lower than trash.

He stops in the doorway and points his finger at me.

"I can't believe you'd take advantage of her like this. You're the last person I thought I'd need to protect her from."

Chapter Seventeen

Josie

Sasha follows me downstairs to the kitchen. We glance at each other as Gabe's voice gets louder and louder. It's hard to make out what he's saying but it's pretty clear he's pissed. I hear the words *fucking tribute* and cringe. Sasha glances back at the stairs and then crosses her arms.

Geez, this is awkward.

"You don't think they're actually going to fight, do you?" Sasha asks.

"I hope not."

Sasha looks unsure but then pastes on a bright smile. "They're intelligent men. I'm sure they can handle a disagreement without resorting to violence."

Part of me wonders if I should tell her about all the times they've thrown fists in the past. Sometimes I used to think they fought just to let off steam. I decide to keep that to myself since that likely won't make either of us feel any better. All I can do is try to distract us so I turn my attention to our reason for being in the kitchen.

"I'll get the bacon started if you don't mind mixing up the batter."

"Of course. However I can help."

She accepts the large mixing bowl I hand her and then I line up the pancake mix, eggs, milk, and the butter. She cracks the eggs in the bowl one-handed with an expert twist of the wrist.

"Measuring cup?" she asks.

I point to the cabinet behind her. After she grabs it, she starts measuring out the different ingredients into the bowl. The voices above us get louder and louder.

"Whisk?" she asks, her voice artificially cheerful.

I open the drawer next to me and then hand it to her. After I get out the bacon from the refrigerator, I pull out a skillet.

Then I decide that this is too much. We're not going to just stand in this kitchen and cook like we don't hear the screaming above us.

"This is weird. And I feel like I should be apologizing to you. You're engaged. This is supposed to be a happy time." Not to mention the fact that Gabe's reaction has to look way out of bounds to anyone not familiar with the dynamics of our weird friendship.

She waves that away. "It's not your fault."

"I know but still... I didn't think he would be this mad. Zack has been worried about this for weeks and it's been really stressing him out. I thought he was overreacting. I guess not."

Sasha sighs. "Gabe thinks of you as the sister he never had, Josie. We've had some pretty in depth conversations about it because honestly, I wasn't convinced you were just friends in the beginning. He really had to explain it to me. But family is important to him and he considers you family. They haven't had many people they can count on so the ones they let in are sacred."

That makes me feel warm inside even if it doesn't make the current situation any easier to handle.

"So I'm guessing Zack is treating you right? You're glowing," she teases.

"I am?" My hands cover my cheeks. I feel giddy, like a teenage girl again. I want this to work out so badly.

Loud footsteps on the stairs prevent her from answering. Gabe appears in the doorway, his chest heaving. His cheeks are still flushed with anger. He glances at me quickly and then turns to Sasha.

"We have to go. Jo, I'll see you later."

Sasha gives me an apologetic look and then rushes after Gabe. I sigh and turn off the heat under the skillet. I climb the stairs and when I push open the door to my room, Zack looks up. He's sitting on the bed with one hand in his hair. When he sees me, his expression closes up. I know him too well for that by now.

"Don't even try to tell me it's okay. It's not okay. But we'll get through it."

He sighs and then opens his arms. I cuddle up on his lap and rest my head on his chest. The steady thump of his heart is reassuring. No matter how bad things ever get, this right here is what will get us through.

"He's never looked at me like that before," he whispers.

I pull back slightly to see his face. Hurt, confusion, anger and sadness are all in his face. It makes my heart break alongside his and it also makes me feel guilty. My love for Zack wasn't supposed to ever cause him pain.

"I never wanted to come between you guys."

"You aren't between us. Gabe has always thought of you as being under his protection. Now you're mine and that changes things a bit."

I scoff. "So what, he thinks you *stole* me away from him? Do I suddenly not have a brain and the ability to think for myself?"

Zack shifts uncertainly. "I don't think you're going to like the answer to that question."

I stand, unable to be still anymore. This makes me so agitated that I want to kick something. I adore Gabe but his tendency to treat me like I'm fragile or incapable of making my own decisions is infuriating.

"Just tell me what he said."

Zack sighs. "Since you just broke up with Perry, he thinks I'm taking advantage of your sad, confused state to get in your pants."

The truth is even worse than what I was imagining. Several things pop into my head but I'm too pissed to even get them out.

Zack seems to sense my rage because he grabs my flailing fists and squeezes until I let out a huff.

"He just needs to adjust to the way things are now."

He sounds confident but I'm not so sure. What if this causes a rift between them that never mends? A break isn't always caused by something huge. All it takes is one small crack in a pane of glass. One crack and the entire thing shatters.

And once broken there are some things you can never put back together again.

———

Zack doesn't leave until after we finish cooking breakfast. I wish he didn't have to ever leave but there are vital things he needs from home. Clothes, his insulin and his keys to the shop. He's planning to pack a bag so he can stay here for a few days at least. Not that Gabe would kick his own brother out in the street but he figures it's a good idea to give them both some time to cool off so they don't say things they can't take back.

I think that's a good idea.

Jamie comes down right before lunch. His hair is sticking up in the front and he looks hungover.

"What was all that racket this morning?" he asks.

"Ugh. Long story."

He eyes me as I pour myself another cup of coffee and then collapse at the kitchen table. I rest my head on my arm. It's not even noon and I'm exhausted. It feels like I've lived a month's worth of drama in one morning.

"Did I hear Gabe's voice this morning or did I dream that?"

"You heard him but it was more like a nightmare. He came over unexpectedly and then cussed Zack out because he found out about our secret relationship."

Jamie gapes. "Wait, it was a secret? So was Gabe jealous or something? I know you guys used to be pretty hot and heavy back in the day, right?"

I sigh. "No, we weren't. That's part of that long story I mentioned."

Jamie tilts his head, seeming to make a decision. He gestures for me to get up.

"Let's take a walk. I need to get some fresh air and you can tell me this long, fascinating story."

"It's cold outside," I grumble but get up and follow him to the front door.

"You've got enough hot air saved up to keep us warm. Come on."

He waits while I put on my shoes and slip into a thick down jacket. He puts on his own coat and then winds one of Isabelle's scarves around his neck. I follow him out and down the drive. It's a nice day, cold but crisp, and the sharp air clears my head instantly. Our neighbor across the street, a widower Izzie has known since she was a toddler, waves at us from his seat by his living room window. We both wave back.

"Nice neighborhood," Jamie observes. "Izzie really likes it here."

I'm glad to hear that he and Izzie have been getting along better. My brother can be stuffy and rigid in his ways sometimes but he's a really good listener. I decide to tell him that.

"I'm glad you're back for a while. I miss having you around as a sounding board."

"I'm glad I'm back, too. Things were different in New York. I changed and not into a person that I was proud of."

"You're making changes that you can be proud of now. That's what counts."

He smiles at me and bumps my arm affectionately. "Enough stalling. Tell me what's really going on with this sordid, brother against brother love triangle you've got going on."

I snort. "It's not a love triangle at all. Gabe and I were always just friends despite the fact that everyone else wanted us to be together."

"Wow, I never even knew that."

"You weren't the only one. Zack believed it, too. All I wanted for years was for him to notice me and now that he finally does, Gabe assumes that he's taking advantage of me or something."

Jamie doesn't say anything but seems to be mulling it all over. I want him to say something, tell me that I'm right to be so angry.

"I just can't believe that Gabe is being such a douchenozzle about this!" I continue.

He snorts out a laugh. "A douchenozzle?"

"Yes," I laugh, too. "He should be ashamed for even thinking that Zack would hurt me. I hate feeling like I'm caught between them. Because if it comes down to a choice, I'll choose Zack."

Jamie looks over at me in surprise. "This thing with Zack, it's really that serious?"

"Yeah. I've been in love with him forever. If it hasn't worn off yet then I don't think it's going to."

We walk along in silence, our breath puffing around our faces in frosty clouds. Even though I didn't want to take a walk, the exercise is helping. Problems don't seem so big out here. My stress level goes down a little. Even though this was a pretty crappy way for Gabe to find out, he'll get used to it eventually. Jamie's next words tell me that he's come to the same conclusion.

"I don't think Gabe is really angry. He's worried. He cares about you. You've been friends a long time."

"Yeah, I hear what you're saying. But a real friend would want me to be happy. I can't be happy without Zack. He should understand. He feels the same way about Sasha."

"What if it was the other way around? If you were in his position it wouldn't bother you at all?"

"No, of course not. Why would it?"

"So, if I told you I liked Isabelle, you'd have no problem with it?"

"Why would I?" I insist.

"Great. Because Isabelle asked me not to go back to New York. And I want to stay."

I stop walking. Jamie walks a few steps before he realizes that I'm not next to him anymore. He turns around and then sighs.

"What? Wait... you're serious? You aren't just saying that to make a point?"

"No. I'm not."

It makes me feel like the worst person ever that my first thought is whether Isabelle just jumped him because he was so readily available. Jamie has been through a lot over the past year and he hasn't been in a great place emotionally for a while. And Isabelle, well ... she's Isabelle. I'm not sure how I feel about this. She's flighty and fun and doesn't take much seriously. She's the exact opposite of what I would have imagined my studious, hardworking brother would go for.

Is it wrong that my first instinct is to protect him?

"Realizing that you're a hypocrite isn't fun," I say finally.

Jamie chuckles. "We weren't trying to deceive you, Josie. Or leave you out. It's just so new between us. I'm having fun for the first time in a long time. And I think this is something special for her, too. I want to see where it goes."

"I'm happy for you, James. Really and truly happy."

He smiles and it's so unlike him, a little bashful and innocent in a way that I'm not used to seeing him. "Really? You don't think I'll screw it up? I've screwed up a lot of stuff in my life so far."

"Not this. I think the two of you are going to be good for each other."

We walk along arm in arm until he glances over at me. "What are you going to do about Gabe?"

"I have no idea. But I'm hoping he's as reasonable and enlightened as I am."

He snorts. It feels good to laugh with him again. Although I would have never in a million years thought Isabelle would be a match for him, there's no denying that my brother is happier than I've ever seen him.

"So, you and Izzie? This is going to take some getting used to."

———

When we get to the house, Izzie is in the kitchen. Jamie takes off his coat and doesn't even bother to hang it on the rack. He just walks right up to her and lifts her off her feet.

"James, what are you doing?" She glances over at me nervously.

"It's okay. We're officially out of the closet, baby." He kisses her right there in the kitchen, like he hasn't seen her in years.

When he sets her down, she sways into him like she's a little dazed. The look on her face when she leans into him is pure love. I've known Izzie for years and I've never seen her look at anyone like that. I'm saddened to think that they were hiding this for fear of my reaction. Especially since I know how hard it is to hide how you feel, fearing how your loved ones will react.

"It's okay. Jamie told me everything."

"I hope not everything," she whispers to him.

The dirty smile on his face makes me laugh. I may have thought that Isabelle was too wild for him but it sounds like there are some hidden layers to my conservative older brother. Whatever the case, there are some things a sister doesn't need to know.

"I'm sure he left some stuff out but I won't ask about it. And you are never, *ever* to tell me."

"Got it," she replies happily.

"But I'm happy for you. Both of you."

She walks over and pulls me into a hug. Jamie watches us with a relieved expression on his face. I can tell that he was really worried about how I would act around Izzie. But I'm truly thrilled. She's been like a sister to me for so long that in a way, he did what I couldn't do. Brought us even closer.

I whisper to her, "Maybe one day we'll be sisters for real."

"Oh Josie, I would love that," she whispers back.

She starts squealing in my ear and I have to laugh because her reaction is just so ... Izzie. Wild, untamed and one hundred percent real. Family events are going to be way more entertaining now. The thought makes me smile.

"Just wait until he brings you home to our parents."

Izzie groans. "We're not that brave yet."

I leave the lovebirds snuggling in the kitchen to go back upstairs. They look like they could use the time alone and honestly, my emotions are a little too raw for me to be around all that happiness. Right now, Zack is gathering his stuff from Gabe's house and probably regretting ever getting involved with me. His relationship with his brother is on shaky ground and who knows if this will affect the business they own together. Being with me has torpedoed every major area of his life.

He probably wishes he'd left me to the Magic Mike auditions that day.

An hour later, Zack enters my room carrying a duffel bag over his shoulder and wheeling a rolling suitcase behind him. At least he's not sporting a black eye or bruised knuckles so I know he wasn't fighting.

"How did it go?"

He glances down at the suitcase. *Stupid question, Josie.* Things couldn't have gone too well or he wouldn't be bringing half his earthly belongings to my house. He reads the trepidation on my face because he taps me under the chin and says, "It will all blow over eventually."

"That bad, huh? Well, you tried to warn me that this would happen."

I take the duffel bag from him and place it on the foot of the bed. He rolls the suitcase into my walk-in closet. Then he stretches out on his side of the bed facing me. We rest there quietly just breathing together. His eyes meet mine.

"Do you regret it?" I ask quietly, hating how scared I am of his answer.

He takes my hand and pulls me closer. I snuggle right under his arm. I love being this close to him.

"Listen to me, sweetheart. When I was a little boy, I was hospitalized several times. I usually roomed with kids who didn't have chronic diseases. Maybe they broke an arm or had their tonsils removed. The important thing to me was that they got to go home and be normal after their hospital stay."

He pauses in the middle of his story and I glance up, surprised to find that he's obviously getting emotional.

"I envied those kids. There were so many times when I wished we could change places. It made me feel ashamed when I thought about how Gabe or my moms would feel if they knew."

"I'm sure they would have understood."

Zack keeps everything so locked down that it's easy to forget that he's had a pretty rough road in the past. Between their financial difficulties growing up to the complications from his diabetes, a lesser person would have emerged bitter and sullen. Instead, he built a business and has been a rock for the rest of his family.

My admiration for him grows every day.

"I'm sure they would have," he continues. "But I can't deny I've felt that a few times even when I was an adult. How much easier would my life have been if I'd been born into a normal family or even an unconventional family with money?"

"But then we never would have met."

His eyes shift over to mine. "You're right. And that would have been a tragedy. When I saw that book of photos you have of me, that was the first time I felt like someone thought

I was worth noticing. I saw myself through your eyes and I'm not broken or defective."

"You're perfect, Zack. Perfect for me."

He kisses me and by the time he raises his head we're both breathing hard.

"I could never regret you. You showed me I'm exactly who I'm meant to be and I'm loved exactly the way I am."

Chapter Eighteen

Zack

Things are tense over the next two weeks. At the shop, Gabe mainly ignores me and everyone has noticed the tension between us. I've been texting Sasha every time I need to drop by to pick up stuff and she must be warning Gabe because he's always gone by the time I get there.

I've brought most of my stuff to Josie's place at this point so I don't have to go back there too often. I feel bad for Sasha because the stress of running interference has to be wearing on her. The last time I was there, she hugged me so tight, like she was afraid it would be the last time.

Maybe I'm afraid it was, too. I was so sure that this would blow over and Gabe would see reason. We'd both apologize and move on. But I've never gone this long without talking to my brother before. It would be one thing if he was mad and yelling at me but this silence is chilling.

It's like he's already written me off as out of his life.

When I get a call from Debbie on a Wednesday asking us to drop by, I agree even though I don't feel like going out. We've always had a routine where they would come to Gabe's for dinner during the week and we'd go to their house for dinner on the weekends. It made it easier for us working late hours at the garage if dinner was waiting when we got home.

But avoiding Gabe has meant that I've seen less of our moms than usual, too.

As soon as I pull into their driveway and see Gabe's car, I know what's going on. Josie sees it too and she covers my hand with hers. "It's time. Come on, let's just go see what they have to say."

Debbie answers the door and as soon as we walk in, Gabe and Sasha look up from where they're seated on the couch. He looks at me and then looks at Debbie in surprise.

"Yes, we tricked you. We have a few things we want to say." She crosses her arms.

Josie squeezes my arm and then speaks up. "I need a few things from the drugstore. Why don't Sasha and I go run a few errands and leave you all to talk."

"You don't have to leave," Debbie says.

Josie gives her a hug and then Paula. "I think maybe a good talking to from their moms is exactly what they need right now."

Sasha hugs them both also and then they leave. Gabe still hasn't looked at me.

Paula points to the dining room table. "Sit. Both of you. We're going to nip this in the bud."

She sits at one end of the table and Debbie sits at the other. Gabe and I sit across from each other. This is like some kind of bootleg family court they've got going on here.

Debbie clears her throat.

"First, we want you both to know that we love you very much. That's why we've asked you to come here today. Because there is no place for division in this family."

Her voice shakes a little at the end of her speech. She's always been very sensitive to confrontation and anger. It really upsets her. Mediating like this has to be tearing her up inside.

I hang my head a little, ashamed that this feud between Gabe and I has brought stress on our moms. It's like I'm five years old and in trouble for sneaking cookies again.

Paula takes over. "Sasha filled us in a little and the rest we've figured out on our own. But we're very disappointed in the way you boys have handled this."

Gabe sighs. "Mom, we weren't trying–"

"No. You two have done more than enough talking. It's time for you to listen. Starting with the fact that no one else knows your friendship with Josie as well as we do. We've had a backseat view to the whole thing."

She looks over to Debbie. It's obvious they've prearranged how to handle this.

"It's true," Debbie continues. "She was a lonely little girl looking for someone to notice her. We gave her the family connection she needed and she brought joy into all of our lives."

"But she's not a doll you can dress up and show off to your friends," Paula interjects, looking directly at Gabe. "She's a person with thoughts, feelings and yes, *womanly desires* of her own."

I'm pretty sure my face is beet red by now. Gabe and I would probably both agree to a ceasefire right now if we never have to hear either of our mothers talk about "womanly desires" ever again.

"This is almost as bad as the birds and the bees speech from the sixth grade," Gabe mutters with a pained look on his face.

I try but I can't hold back my laugh. My mom glares at me and I smother it with the palm of my hand. No matter how old I get, my mom's death glare is still effective.

"Now, I know you think you're protecting her, Gabe. I know that. And it's sweet that you want to do that. But we've always known that Josie had a sweet spot for Zack."

Gabe looks at his mom in surprise, then glances over at me. "You did?"

Debbie grins. "Oh yes. The little thing was always spying on him and following him around asking him questions. I know it annoyed him at first but I think after a while he liked it."

"Yeah, I did. I still do," I admit.

Gabe doesn't look quite as mutinous now but looks back and forth between all of us like he's considering everything.

"I'm not trying to treat her like a doll or whatever. Maybe I've just been trying to protect her for so long that I don't know when to stop."

I know the admission has to be hard for him. "You don't need to protect her from me. I love her, too. And I always will."

He nods to that. It's slight but I get the message. No more fighting. Our family is more important than either of our pride.

"I'm sorry," Gabe grumbles.

"Me, too. Not for falling in love with Josie but for keeping it from you. I wouldn't have liked to be shut out either."

Debbie beams. "See, that's so much better, isn't it?"

I laugh at her obvious relief. "Yeah it is. And while we're having our little "come to Jesus" meeting, there's something else I want to say. I'm going to get in touch with Max. He's made a lot of mistakes, huge ones that have hurt a lot of people. But I want to talk to him one last time. I think I'll regret it if I don't."

Gabe clenches his jaw. "I guess that's fair."

Debbie pats my arm. "If that's what you need to do honey, I think you should do it."

My mom hasn't said anything which I know means she doesn't like the idea. She's been the most vocal over the years about her hatred for the man who left them both pregnant and alone. But then she surprises the hell out of me by nodding her head.

"I think you should do it, too."

Even Debbie looks shocked.

"Oh don't y'all look so surprised. I can evolve!" She rolls her eyes when we all burst into laughter. "Seriously, I'm starting to think the old bastard actually did us a favor."

"You don't mean that," Debbie scolds.

"Actually I do," Paula replies. She holds out her hands to Gabe and I and we both take them. "After all, it's hard to be mad at the rascal when he left his most priceless possessions here with us."

———

Getting closure from Max turns out to be way more complicated than just making the decision. Tank mentioned he'd gone back to Ireland after Gabe's stabbing but I'd assumed he would be back at some point. He has so many business interests here that it never occurred to me he might not ever come back.

After almost a week of messages back and forth from his lawyer, I'm standing outside his usual suite at the StarCrest hotel, one of the many luxury hotels he owns. I'm not sure how to act around him now that I know the truth. He's a guy who left his kids but he did it for a good reason.

Although I have to shake my head at the idea of Max deliberately knocking up a bunch of women. It's such a twisted sort of logic but I can't deny that his plan worked. He has five sons who all grew up relatively normal and away from the long arm of his criminal family. Which wouldn't have happened if Max had stayed in our lives.

Now that I know more about what he was running away from, I'm not so sure I wouldn't have made the same choice.

When I finally knock, Max answers the door himself. "Come in, Zachary. I'm glad you're here."

"Hey, Max. Thanks for seeing me."

I step inside and follow him into the hotel suite, trying to keep my shock at his appearance under control. Max has been sick the entire time I've known him but he looks like he's aged twenty years in the last few months. He's walking with his cane though instead of using the wheelchair so he must not be doing that badly.

It's quiet in the suite and his usual bevy of assistants aren't hovering the way they usually are. When he's grumpy Max is always threatening to fire them all. Maybe he finally did it. Or maybe he got tired of being surrounded by people who are only there because he's paying them to be.

That's a lonely way to live.

The past few weeks, isolated from Gabe and our little family, have really given me new perspective on Max's life. It must have been really hard for him to break away from everything he ever knew and strike out on his own.

He sits on the couch in the living area and props his cane next to him. Then looks at me with curiosity. I'm the one who asked for this meeting which is a departure from the usual. He went so far as bribing us to meet with him weekly. So I'm sure he's curious why I've brought him here now that he's released us from our obligation.

"I'm sure you're wondering why I asked to see you."

He smiles faintly. "I'm lucky any of you are still speaking to me at all. After everything that's happened, I figured we'd reached the end of our road together."

"I'm still upset about what happened to Gabe. And your part in it. But I've gotten a few reminders lately that life is short and nothing is guaranteed. You're my father, the only one I'm going to get and there are a few things I want to say to you."

"I'm listening," he says quietly.

I clear my throat, more nervous than I expected to be.

"First, I'm not even mad at you for leaving our moms. I understand why you did it but I am pissed that you didn't send money. There were a lot of years when we could have really used it."

He listens quietly, not interrupting or defending himself.

"And it sucked that people made fun of us for not having a father but it was worse that you never made any contact at all. Even if you'd been absent, it would have been nice to know something about you other than your name. Tank and Finn had those early years with you but the rest of us got nothing, not even some half-assed Christmas cards."

His eyes close briefly but he still doesn't interrupt. I appreciate that he's letting me get this all off my chest.

"I'm in love with the most amazing woman and she's made me think about a lot of things I take for granted. I'm not sure what any of this means for our relationship in the future but I didn't want to leave anything unsaid. Just in case."

My rambling explanation must make some sense to him because he says, "I'm always happy to see any of my children, Zack. For any reason. Even if it's to accept the many ways I've failed."

That seems a little harsh. Even though I'm mad at him, he has at least tried to make amends. That's a lot more than most men in his position would do.

"You did a few things right. My mom said something that made a lot of sense last week. She said that you left your most priceless possessions behind with them. I wouldn't trade my family for anything so maybe everything worked out the way it was supposed to."

I stand then, not sure I can do meaningless small talk after such a heavy conversation. "I'm going to go. Sorry I made you come all this way just so I could accuse you of a bunch of stuff."

He leans on his cane heavily as we walk back to the front door.

"I'm glad you came for whatever reason, Zack. It means I can tell you this in person. I've decided to start distributing my estate early. I've worked hard and I want to make life easier for my sons sooner rather than later. I was wrong to attach strings to the money, I see that now. You can't hold people to you with iron bars. Not if you expect them to stay."

I'm shocked at how sad his words make me. You would think I'd be happy that he's going to give us the money outright, no strings attached.

No matter how I feel about him, Max's money has given me the security I need and provided an entree into Josie's world. I don't care about the money but I do care about her. It makes it easier for me to take care of her and smooths the way in the world she comes from.

She'd leave all that behind for me, I have no doubt, but thanks to Max's money she won't have to. For that I'll always be grateful.

"Can I hug you, maybe?"

I feel like a pussy for even asking but when he holds out his arms, I go to him instantly, careful not to squeeze too tight. I can still feel the sharp jut of his bones beneath his skin and when I pull back, my eyes are damp and so are his.

Somehow I know this is the last time I'll ever hug my father. And even if he's not saying it outright, it feels like this is one of the last times I'll ever see him.

It feels like I'm saying goodbye.

Chapter Nineteen

Zack

Over the next month, Josie and I settle into a routine. She's finished editing all the photos she's taken of me and her next gallery show is scheduled.

I haven't seen any of the pictures yet due to *artistic integrity* but Josie has assured me that it won't be too mortifying for my moms to come. That makes me feel better because that was a huge blind spot in my plan to pose for her.

I was totally cool with my junk being out there for strangers to view.

My moms, not so much.

On the night of her show, she rides with me over to Gabe's house. It's the first time I've seen her all day since she's been busy with last minute prep and I was off preparing her surprise.

I can't wait to show her later.

We're all meeting at Gabe's house beforehand to toast Josie's success in private since she'll be busy mingling and talking to the buyers at the show. As soon as we walk in, Debbie and Paula start banging their spoons against their champagne glasses.

"They're here! Congratulations Josie!"

My mom is wearing a black dress and black heels that make her look way younger and Debbie has gone for a green dress with shiny sequins around the neck. When she sees us, Sasha starts pouring the champagne.

"I see you guys started without us."

They swat at me playfully before kissing Josie and praising her dress. She's in a fitted white sheath that makes her dark hair and ruby lips the standout. Beautiful as she always is to me, she's even more so when she's happy.

"You both look wonderful. I'm so glad you're coming. These things are always a little crazy and it's nice to have familiar faces in the crowd."

"We're always happy to support you, honey. So, what is this show about? More like last time? Some of those couples shots were pretty hot." Paula fans her face, making us all laugh.

Josie blushes and glances over at me. We haven't told them that I'm the model for her show yet and I'm not really looking forward to when they find out. Even when tastefully done, nudes are nudes. It's still pretty embarrassing.

Gabe enters the room just in time to hear Paula's question. "Yes, what is your show about Jo?" He raises his eyebrows innocently. Next to him, Sasha almost chokes on her drink.

Josie glares at him. "I did something a little different this time. I'm telling a story with pictures. I hope it does well."

"It's going to be great," I tell her.

She leans into my side and smiles gratefully. I'm so proud to support her and stand by her side. Loving her is the greatest privilege of my life and I'm honored to tell her that every day. She should never have even a moment of doubt where her talent is concerned, but when she needs a reminder, I'm here for that, too.

I've even made an effort to reach out to her family, inviting them to dinner at Izzie's one night. They didn't come but I'm not going to give up. It's not fun to hold my tongue around her parents but I'll do it for her. I can play nice to make her happy. Everyone has to make compromises.

Gabe is always telling me that's just part of life. We have some long-time customers that are total douchebags but we appreciate their business so I can't always say what I think around them. Is it really any different for me to hold my tongue, put on a monkey suit and pretend I don't know that Jo's mother hates me?

Josie doesn't know this yet but I invited them to her show tonight. Mr. and Mrs. Harlow probably aren't ever going to be my biggest fans but they seem to have accepted that I'm here to stay.

That's all I can ask for.

After sharing a toast, Debbie and Paula leave for the show. Josie hands me her champagne glass.

"I just need to double check that I remembered to put my business cards in the car. I'll only be a second."

I wander over to the mirror on the living room wall and fiddle with my tie. I'm not used to wearing them and I always tie them too tightly. It feels like I'm strangling to death.

"Here, let me fix it. You always do it wrong." Gabe knocks my hand away and then does something that allows me to breathe a little easier.

He doesn't look at me as he's fixing the knot and I try not to stare at him. But it's hard not to when he's this close. Things have been better with us lately but I still feel the void in my life where he used to be. I have other friends, sure. Reed has been great, taking me out for a beer after work a few times. But nothing can fill the hole where my brother should be.

"First a tuxedo and now this? You really must be serious about her," he comments finally.

"I am. I've never been more serious about anything in my life."

He finally looks at me then. "I really am sorry about everything. I know I went off the deep end a little with the way I reacted. I want to explain it to you but I'm pretty sure I'm going to fuck it up."

"Even if you do, I'll listen anyway."

He claps a hand on my shoulder. "You always give me the benefit of the doubt. Even when I was completely off the rails, you were always there to drag me back."

"I tried to be. You're my brother. We're in this thing until the end."

He smiles at that then blows out a deep breath. I can tell he's gathering his thoughts so I don't interrupt. Gabe is usually the smooth one, the one who always knows what to say. If he's not sure where to begin that speaks volumes.

Finally he puts his hands on his hips and looks over at me. "Do you remember that night when we found her? What am I saying, of course you remember. Anyway, that night ... I swear I could have killed those guys. She looked like she was about twelve and she was so scared. But she took one look at me and assumed that I was there to help her. Everyone else usually assumed that we were up to no good. And we usually were."

I can't help laughing at that. With hindsight, I can understand why a lot of the adults in our community were hesitant about us. We were a couple of badasses, especially during our teen years.

"Josie was the one thing that I could get right. I could protect her, keep her safe and somehow it made me feel like I was atoning for all the wrong I've done. I've hurt a lot of people but with her..." He glances over at me then shrugs. "With her I had a chance to start over. It was the first time that I'd had someone assume the best. She made me want to live up to that."

"I get it. I feel that way about her, too. But with her, it's not just that she makes me want to be better but I actually *am better*. I would have never thought I was capable of loving like this."

Gabe grins. "That's how I feel about Sasha. It's a powerful thing. Welcome to the ball and chain club."

We laugh together.

"Don't let Sasha hear you say that."

"Naw, I'm not scared of her." He glances behind him at the open door. "Much."

Things are back to the way they should be. It feels good to have my brother in my corner again. The tension between us was bothering me more than I wanted to admit. We've always been a unit, Gabe and I. Even though things are changing now I never want to lose the bond we have.

"It's a good thing that you finally invested in a tux, bro. You'll need it soon anyway," he says.

"Why is that?"

"I need a best man at my wedding."

I hit his shoulder. "I've got your back. Always."

Chapter Twenty

Josie

Zack was quiet on our ride to the gallery which makes me think that he's just as nervous as I am. Taking photographs of him is something I've been doing for years so I'm confident the shots on display are exceptional. Few people have more knowledge of how to shoot Zack Marshall to best advantage than I do. But the story told by my pictures is one that's not only erotic but wistful and hopeful, too. As well as intensely private.

Once everyone sees what I've done with the show, all my feelings for him will be out there exposed to the world. I can only hope I made the right decision.

Because after this exhibit, Zack won't be the only one laid bare.

When we arrive, Zack kisses me and wishes me luck. I take a moment to collect myself and then walk to Mr. Hartwell's office. He asked me to come here before the show. I'll wait in here while the guests arrive and he greets everyone. Then he'll introduce me. This is entirely different from last time when I was just one artist among many on display. This time it's just me.

The whole thing makes me feel like they think I'm a way bigger deal than I actually am.

After only five minutes, my stomach is a mass of knots. My mouth feels like sandpaper and I'm on the verge of dry heaving. Not being able to swallow properly only makes the nausea worse. I'm on the verge of running out of there when the door opens. Gabe enters and hands me a bottled water.

"For your stomach."

I open the bottle and gulp it down gratefully. Then I narrow my eyes at him. "I hate that you know me so well."

He leans against the desk and looks around the office curiously. "This is a big deal, Josie. I'm proud of you."

I slam the water bottle down on the desk next to him. "If you're proud of me then why couldn't you believe that I'm smart enough to pick the person I want to spend my life with?"

He runs a hand through his hair, sending the dark strands into disarray. Funny how I never noticed that both he and Zack do that when they're annoyed.

"When I found out that you were hiring a model, all I could see was all the ways it could go wrong. I was really afraid for you and that's why I sent Zack to stop it. So to find out that he didn't stop it but just inserted himself into the process, well, I jumped to a lot of conclusions and made a lot of judgments I shouldn't have. I'm not proud of that."

"It really upset me that you assumed I can't make my own decisions."

He makes a face. "It's been pointed out to me that I'm treating you like a doll. Or something. Anyway all the other women in my life have pointed out the error of my ways. Repeatedly."

"Well good. That really hurt him that you thought he'd take advantage of me. And for the record, Zack didn't have to trick me into falling for him. I fell a long time ago."

He picks at the edge of the desk. "I just had to know that he wasn't hurting you. I promised that I'd never let anyone hurt you again. And that promise I made to you has reminded me of the kind of person I want to be over the years. I owe you for that."

I shake my head, moved by what he's said. "You don't owe me anything. We're friends. That's part of the job."

Because I know he won't make the first move, I walk over and hug him. "I love you Gabe but the next time you pull that crap I'm going to kick your ass."

He bursts out laughing. "Duly noted."

"So did you get a chance to walk the exhibit?"

"The pictures are fantastic, Jo. Really amazing." He sounds awed.

"Really?" My voice is small and I know he can tell that I need the reassurance.

"Yeah. I told Zack that I was sorry before we came here tonight but I'd have said it anyway after seeing this. You really love him, don't you?"

"I do. It's always been him. Even when he had no idea and made my life hell every day."

He laughs. "You guys did have some arguments for the ages. Hopefully that means you've gotten it all out of your systems."

I recall our passionate lovemaking the night before. Zack usually takes me nice and slow until I feel like I'll die before I get what I need but then there's the times when we're going at each other furiously. Almost like angry sex.

"I hope we never get it all out of our systems."

Gabe pretends like he's sticking his finger down his throat. "I don't want to know."

I laugh at the look of disgust on his face. "I told Jamie that you were being a douchenozzle about this whole thing."

That makes him crack up. "I love that. I'll have to start using that one."

We're still laughing when the door opens again. Mr. Hartwell gestures to me. "It's time, Ms. Harlow. Are you ready to meet your adoring fans?"

Gabe hugs me and then pushes me toward the door. "Go, be fearless."

"Thanks, Gabe."

I follow Mr. Hartwell out of the office and down the hall. When we enter the main gallery, he accepts a microphone from someone. When he calls my name, I'm nearly deafened by the applause. But all I'm doing is looking for the only face in the crowd that matters.

Zack.

When I see him, I smile and revel in the spotlight.

———

I'm in the middle of talking to a potential buyer when I see them. My parents. My mouth falls open and I stop speaking mid-sentence. The buyer stops talking too and glances around us, trying to figure out what I'm staring at.

"Would you excuse me?"

I don't even wait for an answer before I walk away. My brother and Izzie are here somewhere but I doubt he would have told my parents. They've been just as dismissive of his relationship as they've been of mine. If he'd known they planned to be here, he would have warned me for sure.

My mother sees me coming first. She's standing in front of one of the early pictures in the series, from when Zack and I first decided to take this journey together. We were walking and I'd just told him that he was my first kiss. The look of awed wonder on his face contrasted with the barren trees behind him is quite striking. I titled the image, *The Revelation*.

"Josephine."

"Mom? Dad?" I'm staring like I'm not sure it's really them. "What are you doing here?"

Mom folds her hands in front of her, looking extremely uncomfortable. "Zack invited us. We didn't even know you had another show."

"He did? I didn't know he was going to do that."

Now I'm really confused. My parents haven't ever been particularly welcoming to Zack so the idea of him inviting them anywhere is pretty weird. And why the hell wouldn't he warn me?

"Please don't be angry with him. He wanted us to know how proud he is of you. He told us that if we could come and be supportive that it would mean a lot to you." She smiles tightly.

I'm surprised they came. They always seem like being around me stresses them out more than anything else. As the silence stretches into awkwardness, I realize it must seem like I don't want them here which isn't true at all. I just want them to *want* to be here.

"I would have invited you but I was pretty sure you barely recovered from just hearing about the last one."

My mom's lips tilt up slightly. Did she just smile? I'm starting to feel like I'm in some sort of alternate dimension. Is my mother really hanging out at an erotic art show and smiling?

"Well, pumpkin. I'm going to take a little walk around. I'll see you later." My father kisses me on the cheek.

After he's gone, my mother smiles nervously. "Your father is a little bashful about this whole thing."

"I'm just surprised he came at all."

"Is it okay that we're here?"

She sounds uncertain and it's unlike her. Although honestly her being here in the first place is wildly out of character so I probably shouldn't be shocked by anything that happens tonight.

"Yes. I'm happy you're here."

It's true. Even though it's kind of embarrassing it's also really sweet that they came to support me. All I've ever wanted was for them to *see* me. Even if they weren't proud, if they just noticed that I was a unique person with hopes and dreams different from theirs, that would have been enough.

Maybe this can be a new start. For all of us.

"I really appreciate that you guys came to support me. You don't have to stay though. I'm sure this isn't your thing."

"Actually I've been quite surprised tonight. Your pictures are simply stunning, Josephine. You're very talented."

"Thanks, Mom."

I'm sure she's just saying that. While I have no idea what Zack said to them to get them here tonight, it must have worked. They're here and making an effort to be supportive. I couldn't have known how much it would mean to me until it actually happened.

She must read the disbelief on my face.

"I'm not just saying that because you're my daughter. Your work really commands the eye. Even the more racy images are tastefully done. Looking at these, well, it reminds me of when I was young and in love. Your Zachary is quite a handsome man."

"Yes, he is." I follow her gaze to the picture behind us.

"He really loves you, Josie. He asked us to come because he thought it would make you happy. It's a wonderful thing to have a man who loves you that much. He really thinks you hung the moon. I can see now that you've done just fine ignoring my advice."

She glances back at my father. "Maybe I could take a few pointers from you."

In an impulsive move, I hug her. "I think there's a few things we can learn from each other."

After a brief pause, her arms come around my back. "I think you're right."

We stay just like that, embracing in the middle of the crowd, neither of us wanting to break the connection. For the first time in years, she isn't my critic she's just my mom.

And that's all I need.

———

After leaving my parents talking with Debbie and Paula, I walk around the edges of the exhibit. I see Mr. Hartwell coming my way so I turn and wait until he passes. I've done my duty tonight and played nice with all the influential critics and buyers. Now I need to find Zack.

His reaction, after all, is the only one I really care about.

I start at the beginning of the exhibit with the picture he found that day in my secret album. He looks so young and it's something of a shock when compared to the later images in the show but I wanted it there for a reason. The people in our lives who know us personally will understand what it means.

That I've loved him that long.

I decided to call the exhibit *Falling in Stages* because that's how I fell in love with Zack. It was such a gradual thing that I didn't even know it was happening until it was done. I imagine it's like drowning. You don't know you're in trouble until you're already in too deep.

I walk the timeline, looking at every picture with new eyes. In the early shots his face shows mistrust, fear and annoyance. Then it changes to affection and playfulness as we romp our way through a series of adventures. Then there's the incredibly vulnerable images I took while he was ill. It was the day I pricked his finger for him and he made the joke about not pulling the plug. The way he's looking at me, it's like he's afraid to believe anyone could love him that much.

Finally, I come to the last image. The capstone of the show. It's from the night he told me he loved me for the first time. This picture is one of the most erotic in the show but also one of the most intimate. He's wearing nothing but a towel slipping low on his hips and the most adoring expression in his eyes. Anyone looking at this knows this is a man who loves with his entire soul.

"You made me look good."

At the sound of his voice, I turn and throw my arms around him. "Zack!"

All the emotions from walking the exhibit and seeing the timeline of our love affair gather inside until I fear they'll burst and gush all over him. Not that I think he'd mind. He loves how open I am with my feelings and that I'm not afraid to share them with him. I can only hope he's okay with how I've chosen to share them with the world.

"I've been looking for you. I wanted to see what you think."

He glances behind me at the capstone image. I decided to call it *Fallen*.

"I think it's phenomenal. I am truly humbled by your work."

"Thank you."

Relief makes me almost lightheaded and I jump into his arms again. He swings me around until I'm dizzy with love and pride. I can consider the show a success now no matter how many of the images sell.

"We've definitely gone public now, baby. Anyone looking at these pictures can tell exactly how I feel about you. I'm really wearing my heart on my sleeve here. Metaphorically speaking since I'm naked. Speaking of nudity," he glances down at me. "You didn't use any of the actual nudes."

There are a few shirtless photos from the first day when we did the test shots and of course, in the final image he's only wearing a towel. But for the most part the focus is on his eyes and face. So far the response has been extremely positive. Mr. Hartwell mentioned that one of the reporters called it a "visual romantic journey" so he's positive we'll get some good press as well as a lot of sales.

Since the show was billed as an erotic exhibit, I've been thrilled that people aren't disappointed with the relative tameness of the photos.

"I couldn't do it. You're perfect but I decided that I didn't want anyone else seeing you like that. That's just for me."

He gives me that private smile that never fails to make me want him. "Yeah it is. It's all for you. Whenever you want it."

"I'll want you always, Zack. And I'll love you even longer than that."

Chapter Twenty-One

Zack

Josie and I walk hand in hand from the gallery. The valet brings the car around and as we drive off, she rests her head against the window. I can tell she's still on a high.

The owner of the gallery came to her toward the end buzzing with excitement. The show sold out again and he received a lot of inquiries about private commissions. Even though she's playing it cool, I can tell how excited she is. Her eyes are shining and there's a bright flush to her cheeks.

It thrills me there are more surprises in store for her tonight.

At the next stoplight, I reach into my pocket and pull out a handkerchief.

Josie lifts her head and eyes it skeptically. "I'm a little tired for kinky games right now."

"Now you're making me wish I'd thought of that." I laugh at her chastising look. "Settle down, sweetheart. I have a surprise for you."

"What kind of surprise? Where is it?" She looks around excitedly.

"You have to wear the blindfold if you want it."

"Ok, fine. But it had better be good." She snatches the handkerchief from my hand and ties it loosely behind her head.

"You're a demanding little brat sometimes."

"You love it," she replies breathlessly.

She knows I do.

I take the next turn and then navigate the route I've only been on a few times. The house at the end of the lane is lit up from within so I'm confident that it's been prepared to my wishes. It's two stories with the same sort of old-fashioned Victorian charm she loves about Izzie's place. It also sits parallel with the same river that runs right behind Gabe's house. That was one of the things I knew she'd love as much as I do. We're close to our families.

I park in the drive and then rush around to open her door. I put one hand behind her head so she won't bump it while getting out of the car.

"Zack? Are we there yet?"

"Yes, we are. Damn you're impatient, woman!"

She giggles and bounces up and down right where she stands, her breasts bouncing against my chest. I bite my lip. We need to get this unveiling underway because if she keeps rubbing up against me, I'll have to throw her over my shoulder and take her inside before she even sees where we are.

"Okay, are you ready?"

"Yes!"

I pull the blindfold off gently. Josie blinks rapidly as her eyes adjust. When she sees the house, her mouth falls into an adorable little *oh* of surprise.

"This is gorgeous. Is this one of those cute little bed and breakfast places that we were looking at the other day?"

"No, it's not."

When I don't say anything else she wrinkles her nose at me. God, I love this woman. She makes everything fun.

"Ok then. Where are we?" she asks finally.

"Home."

I watch her face to see the moment it sinks in. It's worth the wait. Her eyes go soft and her mouth curls up into a little smile. "This is ours?"

"It's ours. Welcome home, sweetheart."

She stands on tiptoe and our lips meet in a soft, sweet kiss. Her fingers curl into my jacket as she pulls me closer.

After a moment, she glances over at all the lights on in the house. "Is someone here?"

I pull out the keys I got from the realtor earlier today. Finn's fiancée, Rissa, owns a full-service cleaning company so after all the requisite paperwork was completed, I hired her team to clean the entire house, furnish the main level and even stock the refrigerator for our arrival. Movers brought over the contents of my bedroom and I brought over some of Josie's things this afternoon so we could spend the night.

Our first night in our new house.

She *oohs* and *aahs* her way through the entire first floor and up to the second. After we finish touring the whole house, we end up back in the living room looking out at the back-yard. It's dark so it's hard to make out the river but you can just see the moonlight glinting off the water.

The place was renovated by the previous owners but I have every intention of customizing everything to our own tastes. This will be the house where our lives unfold, where we make our future children, where we make our memories. I want it to be perfect. When I tell her that, she kisses me again.

"You're here. I'm here. It's already perfect."

I can't argue with that.

———

When I lead her back up to the master bedroom, Josie turns to me with a wicked look. She was surprised earlier when she saw that it was already furnished. My bed looks slightly too small for the room so we'll definitely need to buy new. But it works just fine for what I have in mind.

"I see what's really going on here now. This is the real reason you've brought me here." She wags her finger at me and the prim gesture instantly makes me hot.

"What do you mean? It's our house so we can do whatever we want."

I pull her coat off and it falls to the floor at her feet. Mine lands next to it. Then I start unbuttoning my shirt casually.

Josie reaches behind her and unzips her dress and then lets that fall to the floor, too. After shucking out of my shirt, I circle behind to help her take off her bra.

"What do you think we should do our first night in our new place alone, sweetheart? In our new place where there's no one downstairs to hear us." I kiss the side of her neck.

"We could watch television." She sighs as my lips move to her ear.

"Oops, I forgot to tell the movers to bring that."

"Right. We could start decorating the place." Her voice breaks when my fingers find her tight nipples. I roll them into tight points.

"I don't feel like unpacking tonight." My tongue dips into the shell of her ear and she shudders.

"Or you could stop teasing me and make love to me in our new room."

I lift her and carry her to the bed. "Happy to oblige, my love."

We fall on top of the covers in a tangle of limbs, kissing and touching everything we can reach. Josie cries out with abandon, shamelessly riding my fingers, her little cries exciting me until I'm so hard I could drill through the bed.

We're finally free to make all the noise we want and I love it. When I finally pull her panties off with my teeth, I can tell she's already on the edge. Unable to wait any longer, I pull her beneath me and thrust hard.

It barely takes two strokes before she comes, her loud scream pulling me into ecstasy with her.

I roll over and gather her into my arms. Facing each other, we rest quietly until we've both caught our breath. I can't believe this is my life and that we can do this whenever we want. It feels like a dream and I take a moment to be grateful.

Then Josie's stomach growls loudly. Her eyes widen and we both burst out laughing.

After that, I take pity on my poor, overworked baby and we indulge in a naked midnight snack. Rissa left sandwich fixings and an assortment of fruits and cold pasta salads for us to choose from. There's also wine and champagne. Finn wasn't kidding when he said the woman was thorough.

We share a glass and toast our new home.

Then suddenly Josie looks over at me. "I almost forgot. I have a surprise for you, too."

After I show her the clothes I brought for her, she changes into sweats and a T-shirt and then puts her coat back on. She grabs the car keys from the kitchen counter and I watch from the doorway as she retrieves a large wrapped canvas from the trunk.

"When did you put that in there?"

"This morning. You're not the only one who can plan a surprise. Although I have to admit, it's kind of perfect that you'll be unwrapping it here."

I follow her back up to our room and she drops her coat on the floor again. Then she pats the side of the bed, motioning for me to sit beside her. Then she hands me the canvas.

"This is for you."

I unwrap it carefully, leaning it against the side of the bed when I'm done. It's one of the pictures she didn't put in the show. I thought the only ones she held back were nudes, but in this one I'm asleep and half covered by a sheet. It's beautiful.

I'm completely speechless.

She leans over and trails a finger over the canvas. "This picture represents everything I wanted but thought I'd never have. You willingly in my bed every night."

She runs a hand through my hair. I close my eyes and then turn into the caress, kissing her palm.

"I'm definitely willing. And grateful. But I'm surprised you didn't use this in the show. It's amazing."

"I couldn't. For me, this is too personal. This is what I used to dream about. I wanted nothing more than to curl up next to you each night and get to wake up with you each morning."

She looks over at me and her eyes shine with happiness.

"Now you're here and this is really my life. Dreams really do come true."

"You're my dream too, Josie. But the reality we create together is going to be so much better than anything we've ever dreamed."

Josie sighs. "Thank you, Zack. I'm going to love making this a home with you."

———

"*N*ow this is the life."

Tank accepts the beer that I hand him and takes a seat in one of the folding chairs arranged on Gabe's back lawn. He bumps fists with Finn, who arrived ten minutes before and has his bad leg stretched out on another folding chair in front of him.

It's been a few weeks since Josie's show and we've spent the time enjoying the freedom of having our own house. For a while we completely ignored the outside world and just stayed in our own little nest, christening every part of the house just because we could. I think Josie is just happy that she doesn't have to hold back anymore. There's no one to hear her scream. And making her scream never gets old.

Now that Gabe is feeling better, he wanted to have us all over and for that, Josie and I were willing to come up for air. After I told him about my visit with Max, he's feeling the same way I am. Life is short and there are no guarantees about tomorrow. It's great to get everyone in one place and celebrate all the things that are going right in our lives.

The girls, Josie, Sasha, Rissa and Emma, are standing under the gazebo Gabe had erected just for this event. Josie and Sasha were really happy to have a chance to spend more time with their future "sisters" as they've started calling themselves.

Luke arrives then and we all stand to greet him. Our youngest brother is biracial so he looks slightly different than the rest of us but the family resemblance is still strong. He looks like a tanned version of Tank sometimes.

"You guys remember my mom, Anita."

His mother stands behind him nervously holding a pie plate. Her long braided hair is pulled back from her face and she's wearing an elegant black skirt and jacket. Luke mentioned that she finally allowed him to spend a little money on her and buy her a few presents.

"Hello everyone. It's nice to see you all again," she says.

Finn is instantly on his feet. He kisses her cheek effusively. "Is that my pie? You are an angel. A goddess. *Run away with me.*"

Luke pushes him away. "Dude, again with the hitting on my mom."

Finn takes the pie plate reverently. "It's this damn crackberry pie. It makes me do crazy things."

Debbie and Paula come over and welcome Anita with hugs. Their boisterous enthusiasm seems to be putting her at ease and in that moment I love them more than I ever have. A lot of women would be weird about welcoming their sons half-siblings and assorted family members into the fold but our moms have taken it completely in stride.

Tank shakes hands with Luke. "Glad you made it."

Luke looks uncomfortable. He was reluctant to get too close to us at first but Gabe says we all wore him down.

"Now that you're all here. There's something I wanted to ask you."

We all get quiet as Tank takes a deep breath. "Finn has already agreed to be my best man at my wedding. But I want you all to be my groomsmen. I think it's fitting to have my brothers stand behind me while I make vows."

Gabe holds up his beer. "We'd be honored to. And I hope you'll all do the same when it's my turn. We could do it for Finn if he hadn't snuck off with his bride and gotten married in Vegas."

We found out Finn and Rissa were married when he sent us the pictures. Rissa was a gorgeous bride and they both looked really happy in the shots. I have a feeling that *her* happiness is all that mattered to *him*.

Finn takes the razzing with a smile. "I didn't make my move fast enough years ago and she got away. I wasn't taking any chances this time."

"Congratulations, man. Wow. In sickness and in health, it's pretty deep stuff." Luke claps Finn on the back. "Better you than me."

We all laugh.

Tank sets his beer on the ground next to his chair. "I can't believe that I'm about to vow to the death with someone but

I've never been more sure of anything in my life."

"I'm happy for you guys. All of you." Luke glances over at me. "But it looks like Zack and I are the only sane ones left."

Gabe chuckles. I punch his arm, hard now since I know he's fully healed and can take it.

"Actually I'm not," I admit with a smile.

Josie chooses that moment to come up behind me and wrap her arms around my waist.

"Hey, sweetheart."

"Hey. What are you guys talking about over here?"

She's blossomed over the past month, more secure in our love than ever now that we're not hiding from everyone.

It's been an adjustment, living together so soon. All our years of bickering means we know each other's weak spots. We used to use that information to annoy each other but now we use the knowledge to avoid hurting each other.

Being the steward of someone's heart is a responsibility we both take seriously.

Luke laughs. "It's like that, huh?"

Josie kisses me on the ear before going back to the other girls. Luke makes kissy faces at me as soon as she's gone which make us all laugh. I flip the row of steaks on the grill before sitting next to Tank. He has a tense expression on his face as he looks out over the yard.

"What are you thinking about?"

He tips his head in the girls' direction. "That we're some damn lucky guys."

I snort out a laugh. "That we are."

"And that in a weird way Max is responsible for all of this. He brought us all together, as fucked up as it was, but he'll never even know he did it."

Max left the country again right after I saw him that day. He hasn't called, written or tried to communicate with any of us since. The only connection we have to him are the wire transfers that showed up in all of our accounts over the past few weeks. A total of a billion dollars each.

"When he told me he was going to distribute his estate early, I never actually thought he'd do it."

Tank groans. "He's a crazy old bastard. Now he has me feeling guilty for not going to see him again."

Gabe is quiet, picking at the label on his beer bottle. "I kind of wish I'd seen him one last time, too. It's hard to miss what you never had but I was sort of getting used to the idea of having a father."

Luke doesn't say anything.

Independently wealthy since he started writing software as a young teen, he was the only one of us who could afford to ignore Max's initial offer. The rest of us needed the money for some reason or another but Luke never went to see him. Not even once. He was convinced Max was trouble from the start and as it turns out, he was totally right.

But he has to be feeling some kind of loss right now anyway.

"He came back that time just because I asked him to but he's not going to be the one to reach out again. In his mind, leaving us alone was the greatest gift he ever gave us so if you want to see him, you have to make the first move."

Luke makes a face. "I don't have anything to say to him."

"I didn't think I did either until I was there. But I was mad at him for a lot of years and there were a lot of things I wanted to get off my chest."

"I wouldn't even know where to start." Luke looks glum.

"I told him all the reasons I was pissed off growing up. To Max's credit, he let me say what I needed to say even though it had to be hard to hear. I think you should talk to him. Not because he just dropped a bunch of money on us either but for you. He's not going to be around forever and once that opportunity is gone, there's no going back."

"I hear you, man. I'll think about it," Luke promises.

Tank leans forward. "I heard about the wing of the hospital you and Gabe are building. That's awesome."

"Thanks. We've been consulting with experts on pediatrics and neonatology for information on what's needed. It's a lot of work but it's more than worth it."

Gabe and I share a smile. He knows that I got the idea while trying to impress Josie's parents but he was happy to help me make it a reality. He was right there with me as I suffered through the horror of substandard medical care as a child so it's a personal cause for him as well.

We want it done right so the kids in our town will have access to some of the best medical care on the East Coast.

"If you want, my lawyer can send over what he's been doing for us. Finn and I have been funding a lot of cancer research lately. Our mom is in remission after a long battle but I don't think either of us will ever feel safe until there's a cure for cancer. Hopefully we'll see it in our lifetime."

Luke smirks. "Look at us. Making the world a better place."

He's being sarcastic but I know he's got plans for his windfall too. Finn told me Luke plans to provide technology education for underprivileged kids.

"Making the world a better place sounds good to me. Here's to being better." Tank raises his beer.

My eyes meet Josie's across the lawn. Being better is a motto I can get behind because it's how I feel about my life with her. She soothes my fears, challenges my assumptions and makes me strive for more.

Every day.

We all raise our beers and the sound they make as they connect floats above us. Like we're ringing in a new era.

"To being better!"

The End

... for now

Thank you so much for reading *Zack*. Sign up to be notified the next time I have a sexy new book available HERE.

There's only one hacker alive better than Luke. But he's never met his online BFF. Then while consulting on a hacking case for the FBI, the hauntingly beautiful suspect seems to know a lot about him. Things he's only told one other person... **Order LUKE now so you don't miss it!**

If you're in the mood for a really inappropriate romantic comedy, then **One-click BEG ME now!** Find out what happens when a hotshot ad executive discovers his rooster will only crow for one woman. His competition.

———

Keep reading for an excerpt of LUKE!

LUKE

If I thought that I was going to meet this mysterious woman right then and there, it was because I'd forgotten the snail speed at which everything government moves.

First, I was presented with a bunch of paperwork to sign, basically agreeing not to ever reveal anything that happened. I've already signed this stuff before but I guess they have a different layer of legalese if you're in actual contact with a cyber terrorist.

It's about an hour later when I'm led down another hallway. There wasn't much time for me to review the folder of information on the suspect. I got nothing more than a name.

Sarah Parker.

It means nothing to me.

Agent Walker stops right outside a nondescript gray door.

"We'll be right on the other side of the glass. Don't accuse her of anything but try to get her talking about her mission. Find out what the hell she was looking for and how she even knew where to start."

"Right. Get her talking. I can do that."

He hesitates and then opens the door. I step inside and wait until I hear the gentle click of the door shutting behind me. The knowledge that I'm being watched behind the large mirror on the wall doesn't help my anxiety any.

The table in the center of the room is empty. I turn around, looking behind me. I'm about to bang on the mirror and ask what the hell is going on when I notice her in the corner.

She's small, so small I almost mistake her for a child. A curtain of long, dark hair covers her so completely that all I can see are the tips of her Chucks. They're electric blue.

Then she looks up.

We stay suspended like that for what I hope is just a few seconds before I find enough brain cells to speak.

It's the girl from the rain.

"Hey. What are you doing on the floor?"

Large, dark eyes continue to watch me as I take a seat at the table. I'm trying not to move too quickly or do anything to spook her. She already looks pale. She's probably terrified.

I remember what it was like being interrogated by agents as a teenager. I fear any sudden movements will just freak her out more.

Aware that we're being watched, I'm unsure of how to proceed. Walker said she put my name as her emergency contact. But I'm positive that I've never seen this girl before that day in the rain.

So why would she claim to know me?

More importantly, what could she hope to gain by using my name?

Not too many people know about my consulting with the department in the first place. There's no way she could have known that my name would even work in her favor.

None of this makes any sense.

The FBI is tiptoeing around this innocent-looking little girl when she looks more likely to hack into the Disney servers to get some free Princess shit.

"Hey, why don't you tell me what happened. I'm sure you didn't do anything wrong."

She'd gone back to staring at the tips of her shoes but at my words, her eyes swing to mine. I almost shift backward in my seat at the sudden cunning gleam in her eyes. This is not some innocent little kid.

"Are you sure about that? I'm no angel."

It's the first time she speaks and the soft whisper of her voice sends a little shiver down my spine. Then she leans forward and once our eyes meet again, she smiles.

"Well, I'm an angel online but only after *dark*."

My heart stops in my chest and as we stare at each other, our eyes play out a hundred conversations we can't speak aloud. There's no mistaking the emphasis she put on the word dark.

Except for a few slip-ups when I was a teenager, I've been careful about covering my activities online and there's only one person who has been around long enough and is skilled enough to figure out my real identity.

If she knows about my online alter ego, DarkAngel, then there's only one person she could be.

C7pher.

As soon as the thought occurs, it's disregarded as impossible. Maybe she just happened to choose a strange way of phrasing things.

As if she can sense the shift in my thinking she says, "You always said if I needed you, just call."

In those few moments, my entire world realigns and everything I thought was real becomes a dream. After all, how can you rely on anything if the person you've trusted the most isn't who you thought they were?

I stand so fast the metal chair screeches against the floor. Just before I reach the door, she calls out.

"Luke!"

My hand stills on the doorknob. There's nothing we can say with an entire roomful of agents watching. The conversation that needs to take place between us cannot happen here.

Because no matter how pissed I am, I can never forget that this is the one person who can destroy me.

"Just a minute, *Sarah*. I need to explain to Agent Walker that there's been a misunderstanding."

I deliberately raise my voice and turn toward the mirrored wall. A few minutes later, Agent Walker comes in.

"What's going on, Luke?"

I point at Sarah. "I didn't realize who you had in here. She's not a terrorist. She's a white hat. Top Fortune 500 companies hire her to test their systems. She tries to break in the same way any other hacker would, then provides them with an assessment of their vulnerabilities."

Walker glances between the two of us suspiciously. "So, you do know her? Why didn't you say so?"

"I, uh, didn't recognize the name at first."

Sarah stands then and glances at me. "Luke and I have fallen out of touch recently."

"You were on a job when they grabbed you, right?"

She nods. "But it's all supposed to be confidential so I wasn't sure if it was safe to talk. But yeah, I was hired by a private company to test their security. I had no idea that was a government server until it was too late."

Agent Walker doesn't look completely satisfied but at least he doesn't look quite as hostile.

"Sarah is skilled enough that if she was trying to hack into something unauthorized, she wouldn't have done it without rerouting through some foreign ISP first."

Agent Walker nods as if he has any idea what that means.

"I'm sure Sarah can show you the emails from the company that hired her. That should give the FBI something to go on in tracking these guys down."

"Of course," Sarah agrees quickly.

"And we can go back to my place and catch up."

They both stare at me.

"W-What? Your place?" Sarah swallows and then glances over at Agent Walker. "Right. I am pretty tired."

"Now, wait a minute—"

I hold up a hand. "You would have had me under surveillance when I left anyway. Now you can watch us both together. Look, you know she's not behind this. It was obviously a setup and she's going to cooperate fully. At least let us get some sleep."

I can tell he doesn't like having the decision taken out of his hands but doesn't have a good reason to stop us. And I have no doubt that the look in my eyes is pretty scary right now.

Because I have a mission of my own tonight.

To interrogate the beautiful little liar who has been trolling me for the past decade.

Download LUKE now!

The universe clearly hates me.

I work hard and I like to win. So of course, the only woman that gets me going these days is the one woman I need to avoid like the plague. My co-worker. Rival, she-devil and my competition for the biggest ad account this side of the Atlantic.

When I find out she's never taken a trip to O-town, we make a little wager. Not only will I win the client, but I'll prove to her that multiple O's are not a myth.

We work together all day and fight between the sheets all night. But somewhere along the way, I discover that winning isn't enough.

Excerpt of *Beg Me* © 2018 M. Malone

MILO

Time to get our game faces on.

As we approach the table, everyone stands, and the introductions are made all around. Maybe it's because I'm watching Mr. Lavin so closely that I see how his eyes follow Mya after she shakes his hand and then walks around the table to greet the other members of his team. She knows all of their names, as do I. Then she takes a seat right next to me.

Before I can even sit down, James is already ordering a scotch from the waitress. Then I see why.

Elizabeth is sitting two tables away.

She raises her glass of wine in our direction. I turn to see James give a begrudging wave. I'm not sure if anyone else has noticed her yet, but she's already accomplished her goal. There's no way James can focus completely on the client tonight with his ex-wife sitting right in his line of vision.

Christ.

"Thank you all for traveling to meet with me. I've had this week scheduled with potential investors for months, so it's been helpful that you could come to me while I'm already in the States."

"When do you go back to Italy?" Wallace asks. "I follow you on Instagram. You guys, his page is *lit*. Fast cars, beautiful clothes. You're living the dream, man." He sighs before digging into his salad course enthusiastically.

Andre just laughs. "Thank you. This is our goal, to be as the kids say, *fire*. Why is all of the American slang centered around temperature, I wonder? It used to be that things were *cool*, now they're *hot, fire, bomb* or *lit*. Fascinating. I have an entire team of people who study the social media trends."

James looks like he has no idea what is happening. But I strongly suspect that Wallace in his own unique, bumbling way has just broken the ice for us.

Well, if he's broken the ice, I might as well jump in first. "Mirage employs a lot of talented young designers. It's why our ad campaigns are so on trend. We combine years of experience in understanding what makes people buy with the fresh perspective of different generations."

Mya grins over at me. "Wallace is on Milo's team. He's been with us for almost a year now and graduated from Columbia with honors. He's also an amateur photographer and is pretty popular on Instagram, too."

I glance over at her. *He is?* How does she know all that? Maybe there is something to paying attention in those bull-shit icebreaker sessions at work after all.

Wallace looks shocked, too. "My account has nowhere near the numbers some of my friends have, but I just passed ten thousand."

Mr. Lavin actually looks impressed. "That's quite an accomplishment, especially for a hobbyist." He clears his throat. "I'm happy to meet with you all in person after hearing about you from Mr. Lawson."

James gives him a tight smile. "I'm extremely proud of my team."

"It shows," Andre replies.

Dinner proceeds with the typical pleasantries. Wallace looks a little confused, but I can only pray the kid can hold his tongue. With these types of clients, you never rush right into business. You need to woo them, almost like a woman you're trying to convince to come back to your place after dinner. She's not just going to come with you if you ask within the first ten minutes. She needs you to show her that you're worth her time. Are you going to savor her the same way you do the ten-inch porterhouse on your plate? Or will you rush through the act like a kid scarfing down an ice cream cone?

I can't imagine a man like Andre Lavin scarfing anything. He needs to see that we're not only the best team to take over his marketing but also that we're people he can work with.

We need him to *like* us.

As the waitress is clearing the entrees, Andre looks around the table with satisfaction. "Perhaps it is old-fashioned, but I care to meet with any agencies that work on our marketing directly. It's important that the people crafting our image understand what we're about here at Lavin Fashions."

Everyone instantly ceases their side conversations and pays attention. Now we're getting to the good stuff. The reason we're all here.

"What is your vision of Lavin Fashions, Mr. Lavin?" Mya asks. "I've read the official company mission statement, but I would love to hear it from you."

"Please, call me Andre."

The way he's looking at her makes it seem like he just wants to hear her say his name. My hand sitting on top of the table curls into a fist. It's unsettling that this bothers me. He's just a client, throwing a little charm at the pretty ad executive.

I've seen it plenty of times, and I've had my fair share of clients, male and female, attempt to flirt with me.

None of those made me want to growl in frustration. Or made me worry that Mya might actually want to flirt back.

"It's much more than just the clothes," Andre begins after a brief pause. "Our brand creates the garments that become part of people's memories. And for our newest venture, we're looking for a partner that understands the importance of family, friendship, love."

The woman sitting next to him sniffs. *Cristiane Laveque.* From my research on the Lavin team, I know that she's a top designer for Lavin Fashions.

"Apologies, but this is not a strength of American companies, we have found. So few understand *l'amore.*" She shakes her head ruefully as if the vulgar ways of the American market are just too much.

Mentally, I'm rolling my eyes, but this could be a real obstacle to winning their business. If they think that we're not cultured enough, it will be difficult to change that opinion. Granted, Mirage does plenty of "American" commercials and brands, but it's not like we're all racecars and beer. We have plenty of upper-echelon brands in the jewelry, hotel and entertainment industries.

"I believe Mirage can handle anything. We have such a diverse workforce that all of our clients find someone they can relate to. We also have more women in leadership roles than many of our competitors."

Maybe that'll calm her fears that we don't get *l'amore*. Mya in particular handles a lot of brands that cater to women, including a high-profile lingerie line.

Andre sits back in his chair and seems to be considering her words. "I must admit we've been approached by other firms that are run by people who are married. They understand what brides want."

James sits up straighter. "So, it is a bridal line?"

Andre laughs lightly. "Yes, the rumors are true. Lavin Fashions will introduce a new line called Lavin Bridal next year. It will be a separate division of the company which is why I'm meeting with investors. I didn't want word to get out until it was all finalized."

James looks like he's going to be sick. This is why Elizabeth has been so smug. She must have heard the Lavin group wanted someone who has been through the process of planning a wedding. Just another way for her to rub her recent marriage in James's face.

"I'm sure all the women on our team have mentally planned their dream wedding, even if they aren't married." I send a panicked glance at Mya.

This would be a really good fucking time for her to pipe in with some story of how she's been dreaming of her wedding dress since she was a little girl.

Unfortunately, Andre seems to be following my line of thought because he turns directly to Mya, too. "If you were planning a wedding, for example," he says, "wouldn't you want a wedding planner who was married?"

Mya pauses with her water glass halfway to her mouth. "Well, yes. I suppose I would."

James just blinks. Wallace pauses mid-chew with a piece of iceberg lettuce hanging from his lip. The whole table seems stunned into silence. She didn't mean to say that, and everyone can see it on her face. But in a rare, caught-off-guard moment, Mya has done the unforgivable.

She's been honest.

An awkward silence descends over the table. James takes another gulp from his scotch. Across from me, members of the Lavin team exchange significant glances before taking an interest in their plates. Worst of all, Andre Lavin just looks amused.

While Mya looks devastated.

You know how sometimes you can look back and identify the precise moment you fucked up? Well, later tonight I'm sure I'll be remembering the exact second I pushed us all off the cliff together.

"I agree," I state loudly.

James chokes slightly, and Wallace pounds him on the back. I ignore his panicked look and keep my eyes on Mr. Lavin.

"I agree with Mya," I repeat in case anyone at the table missed it the first time I pushed my career in front of a bus. "Having a married wedding planner would be great. Although I'd be more concerned about the people actually doing the work. That's really what sets Mirage apart."

By now, everyone is staring at me, especially James, probably wondering where the hell I'm going with this.

Mya, however, is watching me with a small, tremulous smile on her face. Like she can't believe that I'm backing her up right now. And damn if that smile isn't what does me in. Because I don't just bet on distracting Mr. Lavin; I double down and take it all the way to the bank.

"Mirage is really the best fit for anything to do with weddings. After all, it's the only agency I know with two team leads that are in love and engaged to be married." I turn to Mya and whisper, "Just go with it."

Then I tilt my head slightly and brush my lips over hers.

MYA

Everyone is staring. I can feel the heat of their eyes on the side of my face. But even that isn't enough to take me out of this moment. This sweet, thrilling moment. My eyes drift closed, and the world falls away.

Milo is kissing me.

If you'd asked me just an hour ago what kind of kisser I thought Milo would be, I'd have said aggressive. He's all about going all-in and getting to the finish line. I would have assumed that he wouldn't care much about the process but rather only about the end game.

I would have been completely and utterly wrong.

His lips are soft, and he feathers them over mine gently, barely touching me. The result is a whispery soft touch that sends chills up and down my spine. Then he lays his mouth over mine and kisses me properly, his tongue brushing softly against mine.

After what feels like several hours but is probably only several seconds, he pulls back. But he doesn't just stop. No, Milo can't do anything simply, not even shocking me to my core with a kiss. Because right after he pulls away, he does this soft little nuzzle, rubbing his nose back and forth against mine.

Why is that my kryptonite? That completely unnecessary little snuggle just takes all the indignation I was building up to and scatters it into the wind. Along with all rational thought.

A throat clears and it's like jumping into an ice bath. If we'd been standing, we'd have probably sprung apart, but instead I grope the table blindly until my hand connects with my water glass. The icy liquid cools my throat but not my lust.

What the hell was that?

Everyone at the table is still eating and talking softly amongst themselves, almost like the last thirty seconds didn't just change the rotational orbit of the planet. Isn't it funny how a certain event can knock you off your feet but seems to have no effect on anyone else? It's like experiencing an earthquake while everyone around you goes on with their lives unaware. Well, everyone isn't unaware. Andre Lavin is watching us carefully.

So is James.

Oh shit.

This is where I should speak up. Tell Mr. Lavin that I cannot wait to see his newest designs, that women everywhere are going to be clamoring for the chance to wear one of his dresses. But I can't because my mind is still muddled, and I can still feel the imprint of Milo's lips against mine.

"You make an interesting point, Mr. Hamilton. Being married is one thing, but to have a couple who are currently planning a wedding designing my campaign would be ideal." Mr. Lavin nods in satisfaction. "I had a good feeling about this firm, but I can see that your reputation is accurate. Professional, innovative and discreet. Exactly what I need."

James looks slightly dazed, the same expression you might wear after you narrowly miss being hit by a cab. He looks between me and Milo and then back to Mr. Lavin, but nothing comes out of his mouth.

Once again, Wallace comes to the rescue. "You can't go wrong with those two in charge, if you're looking for discretion. They've been dating in secret for ages and nobody knew except for me. I mean, I could tell. He stares at her ass whenever she walks away."

The water I just sipped comes back up my nose.

Milo hands me a napkin without missing a beat. "Thank you, Wallace. So, Mr. Lavin, tell us about your vision for Lavin

Bridal in particular."

And so it goes. Milo manages to carry the conversation all the way through the dessert course and then through coffee. Personally, I've never understood the practice of drinking coffee after dessert, but when the waitress comes around, I order some anyway. Maybe the extra caffeine will wake me the hell up.

But I still feel like I'm sleepwalking as James bids the members of the Lavin team goodnight and they promise to be in touch. Wallace is the first to scamper off, probably to go post the selfie he took with Mr. Lavin to Instagram. The thought makes me chuckle, but my throat instantly turns to sandpaper when James approaches.

This entire time, Milo and I have been sitting in silence. I couldn't take the chance of asking any questions where the Lavin team might overhear. But now I wish I'd thought to text him or something so I'd know how we're handling this.

But James doesn't look upset at all. He's practically glowing. It could be all the scotch, but either way, he looks thrilled.

"You two, ah, I should have known. You've done an amazing job keeping your relationship out of the office. Good work. Knew I could count on you." He claps Milo on the shoulder and gifts me with a wide, loopy grin.

Even if I knew what to say to him right now, I don't think I'd have the heart to wipe that smile off his face. Tomorrow is soon enough for him to realize that we've screwed up this deal. Maybe a good night's sleep will make him more lenient when he's deciding whether to fire us.

Milo pulls out my chair for me as I stand, and I follow wordlessly as we leave the restaurant. It's a Thursday night, but as we walk back through the casino to reach the elevators to the rooms, there are so many people out you'd never think it was a weekday. Time seems to move differently here. I notice an older lady with a purple fanny pack methodically feeding coins into a slot machine. She looks like she's been at it for a while. Maybe I should just stay down here, living off the free drinks and the adrenaline of gambling. It would probably be better than what's waiting for me when we get back to DC.

I'm so deep in my thoughts that I'm not paying attention when we get on the elevator. It's only when it stops that I realize we didn't push the button for my floor. But Milo loops his arm around my waist and guides me out of the elevator anyway.

"But my room–"

"Not here," he murmurs in my ear. The deep rumble of his voice so close sends a shiver down my spine. "Some of the Lavin team are on this floor. Wait until we get inside."

"Inside what?" Belatedly, I realize he means inside his room. He has his key card out and the door open before I can say, *No way in hell.*

The door slams shut behind us, and all the things I was getting ready to say get stuck in my throat.

Trying to gather my thoughts, I look around the room. The layout is the same as the one I was given, TV, big window directly across from the door, except he has a king-size bed instead of two doubles. Behind him, there are several dress shirts scattered on the bed, and the covers are all tangled, like he took a nap before coming down to dinner. Just like that I have a mental image of Milo naked in those sheets, and being alone with him in this room seems like a *very* bad idea.

Completely at ease with the idea of the two of us being alone, he shrugs out of his suit jacket and loosens his tie. I'm instantly distracted by the small patch of skin revealed at the top of his shirt where it's unbuttoned. "I know you must have a million questions," he says finally.

But I don't. Truthfully, I only have one.

"What the hell just happened?"

Download BEG ME now
at minxmalone.com/begme

Just One Thing : Scientist Bennett Alexander is a bona fide genius but he still can't figure out how to "get the girl". So he hires a dating tutor. What could go wrong? Other than falling for his teacher, of course.

Bad King: My parents just put a gold diggers target on my back. But if all they want is a wedding, I can do that. I'll find the fiancee of their nightmares. *Who Wants to Marry a Billionaire? Must be completely inappropriate.*

Bad Blood : I'd do anything for my best friend's little sister. Until she asks for the one thing I can't give. One night. No rules. ***2019 RITA® Award Winner!***

Blue-Collar Billionaires

Billions from the deadbeat dad they never knew sounds pretty sweet. Until they find out what he really wants.

Tank / Finn / Gabe / Zack / Luke

- Romantic Suspense -

(Co-authored with Nana Malone)

- The Shameless Trilogy
- The Force Duet
- The Deep Duet
- The Sin Duet
- The Brazen Duet

About the Author

M. Malone is a RITA® Award winner and a NYT & USA Today Bestselling author of completely inappropriate romantic comedy. She spends most days wearing Wonder Woman leggings and T-shirts that she's embarrassed for anyone to see while she plays with her imaginary friends.

She lives with her husband and their two sons in the picturesque mountains of Northern Virginia even though she is afraid of insects, birds, butterflies and other humans.

She also holds a Master's degree in Business from a prestigious college that would no doubt be scandalized at how she's using her expensive education.

facebook.com/minxmalone

twitter.com/minxmalone

instagram.com/minxmalone

bookbub.com/authors/m-malone